"Do you want to know if the baby is a boy or a girl?"

Katya blinked. Did she? She hadn't thought about it in any real sense until now. The baby's sex was just another one of those things she'd kept out of her mind—ha[d] [not thought] about too much. [But with the image shown] in front of her, sh[e had a sudden urge] to know. "Do you[...]"

He smiled at her [and read her mind,] he admitted. Ben had also been surprised by the power of the tiny image on the screen. Feeling the baby kicking had been amazing, but this was so much more incredible. He was going to be a father, and his curiosity to know everything about this tiny, precious human being was incredibly strong.

"Ragazzo," the radiologist said. "A boy."

A son. Katya looked back at the screen again. She was having a baby boy. She felt Ben's hand on hers tighten and saw his crazy grin in profile. He seemed as taken by the image as she. Would her son look like his father? Would he have dark brown eyes, killer eyelashes and a quick, lazy grin?

"There, see," Ben teased. "I told you the baby was fine."

"He," Katya corrected.

Ben nodded and grinned at the wonder in her voice. "Our son."

Dear Reader,

This was such a hard book to write. I had to travel all the way to Positano in Italy to research it. I had to eat the local cuisine (freshly caught seafood and pizzas to die for and, my-oh-my, all that wonderful aromatic basil), drink the local wine, shop in the local boutiques and markets and wander through the narrow, twisting alleys and bougainvillea-draped passages. One day I even had to sit and stare at the gently lapping ocean for hours while I basked in the perfect September weather at a gorgeous little *ristorante* right on Fornillo Beach.

I had to walk the cobbled streets of Ravello and admire the amazing old villas—with their spectacular gardens and grape groves—all perched high in the mountains above the Amalfi coast, with one-eighty-degree views of the gleaming Mediterranean. I had to buy the most gorgeous round mirror with a pretty ceramic-tiled border, and a red coral cameo necklace, handmade by local craftsmen using materials that had been farmed from local waters.

I tell you, Dear Reader—I really suffered for this book!

And I hope all my hardship has paid off. I hope that you find yourself totally immersed in this wonderful region as you read Katya and Ben's much-anticipated story. They were secondary characters in *The Surgeon's Meant-To-Be Bride,* and I knew all along that they had to have their own story. The acid-tongued, poor Russian nurse and the smooth-talking, aristocratic Italian surgeon? I knew straightaway they were meant for each other.

Enjoy,

Amy

THE ITALIAN COUNT'S BABY
Amy Andrews

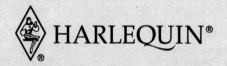

HARLEQUIN®

TORONTO • NEW YORK • LONDON
AMSTERDAM • PARIS • SYDNEY • HAMBURG
STOCKHOLM • ATHENS • TOKYO • MILAN • MADRID
PRAGUE • WARSAW • BUDAPEST • AUCKLAND

If you purchased this book without a cover you should be aware
that this book is stolen property. It was reported as "unsold and
destroyed" to the publisher, and neither the author nor the
publisher has received any payment for this "stripped book."

ISBN-13: 978-0-373-06637-7
ISBN-10:   0-373-06637-6

THE ITALIAN COUNT'S BABY

First North American Publication 2008

Copyright © 2007 by Amy Andrews

All rights reserved. Except for use in any review, the reproduction or
utilization of this work in whole or in part in any form by any electronic,
mechanical or other means, now known or hereafter invented, including
xerography, photocopying and recording, or in any information storage
or retrieval system, is forbidden without the written permission of the
publisher, Harlequin Enterprises Limited, 225 Duncan Mill Road,
Don Mills, Ontario, Canada M3B 3K9.

This is a work of fiction. Names, characters, places and incidents are
either the product of the author's imagination or are used fictitiously,
and any resemblance to actual persons, living or dead, business
establishments, events or locales is entirely coincidental.

This edition published by arrangement with Harlequin Books S.A.

® and TM are trademarks of the publisher. Trademarks indicated with
® are registered in the United States Patent and Trademark Office, the
Canadian Trade Marks Office and in other countries.

www.eHarlequin.com

Printed in U.S.A.

MEDITERRANEAN DOCTORS

Let these exotic doctors sweep
you off your feet....

Be tantalized by their smoldering good looks,
romanced by their fiery passion
and warmed by the emotional power
of these strong and caring men....

MEDITERRANEAN DOCTORS

Passionate about life, love and medicine

To Anna. A fabulous neighbor.
Thank you for Hotel Pasitea.

CHAPTER ONE

Katya Petrova clutched her stomach as the plane hit a small air pocket. Her insides lurched and she felt a flutter down low as the plane continued its smooth journey.

The baby? She kept her hand in place and waited, every cell in her body straining to detect a tiny foetal movement. *Come on, baby.* The seconds ticked by. Nothing. A few more. Still nothing.

Well, duh! She removed her hand impatiently. As if there would be. She was just twelve weeks. The baby was only about ten centimetres long! She had a good few weeks yet, maybe even up to ten according to some books, before she'd feel his or her first movements.

She made a mental note to stop reading books. She needed to stop this fantasy land she kept drifting into. There was absolutely no point getting more attached than she was because there was no way she could be a mother to this baby. No way.

It was bad enough that she already loved the baby more than her own life. She had to toughen up. Stop thinking of it as 'the baby' or 'he' or 'she'. 'It' was so much more removed. And that's what she needed to be—removed. Because she was doing the right thing here. When you loved somebody you wanted the best for them, right? And she was *so* not the best thing for this baby.

And that was why she was here on this plane flying to meet a man she barely knew. To find out if the best thing for the baby was its father.

By the time she disembarked an hour later and had gone through passport control and customs, Katya was feeling so tired and nauseated she wanted to scream. Now she was nearly in her second trimester the vomiting was settling but her extreme state of nervousness was a volatile mix for her delicate constitution.

It had been three months since she'd seen him, three months since she'd done the single most irresponsible thing she had ever done. And they had parted badly. And she was carrying his baby.

Being greeted by flowers did not improve her mood.

'I said strictly business.'

She glared at him, hands on her hips, staring at the massive bouquet of red roses. She could smell their delicate fragrance wafting towards her and pressed her hands harder into the bone and flesh of her hips to stop herself reaching for them.

People jostled past and around them at the busy arrivals gate of Leonardo Da Vinci Airport, eager to greet loved ones. The two of them stood out in the crush, the only two people keeping their distance despite the press of bodies around them. They did not embrace. They did not cry.

Count Benedetto Medici chuckled and feigned a wounded look. Just like he remembered her. Blunt. To the point. Her accented English making the words even more clipped. Someone who didn't know her might even describe her as unemotional. But he knew intimately that under the surface Katya Petrova was an intensely passionate woman. '*Cara*,' he cajoled.

'Do not *darling* me,' Katya said briskly, ignoring the way his voice stroked heat across her skin. That's what had got her into this mess in the first place. Memories of their last night together played like a film in her head. Unfortunately time, distance and weeks of throwing up had not immunised her against his charms or dulled her reaction to the sexy purring quality of his very deep, very male voice.

'But I bought them for you…as a welcome-to-my-country gift.'

Katya sniffed as his beguiling smile did funny things to her equilibrium. 'I am here to work, Ben. There is no need for gifts.'

'They are too beautiful to throw away,' he said softly, thrusting them towards her again.

Katya could smell the crimson blooms and she was, oh, so tempted. But there was a principle here. Flowers were for lovers and they weren't. Once did not count. Ben was a rich, attractive man—aristocracy for heaven's sake—used to getting his own way. But she wasn't here to be a rich man's darling. That was her mother's specialty.

She was here on a fact-finding mission. Just because she couldn't look after this baby, it didn't mean she was just going to let anybody do it. Ben may be the father but she knew so little about him. Yes, he could obviously provide for it. But could he give it the other things?

The intangibles. His love. His time. His devotion. His stories. His commitment. Katya knew too well what it was like, growing up without any of those things. She also knew what it was like growing up without a father. Maybe things would have been different if she had. Maybe not. But she wanted the very best for this baby and next to a mother, surely that had to be the father? And that was what she was there to find out.

She looked around her at the now thinning crowd and

spotted a young man rocking on his feet, anxiously scanning the arrivals corridor. 'Ask him who he's waiting for,' she said, turning back to Ben.

Ben chuckled again. But he did as she asked. There was a brief exchange between the two men. 'His fiancée,' Ben relayed.

Katya smiled. 'Perfect. She'll love them,' she said, and then strode forward, dragging her single suitcase behind her on its wheels, following the exit signs.

Ben threw Katya's medium-sized bag, which looked like it had seen better days, into the boot of his Alfa.

'This is all you brought?' he asked.

'Yes. Why?'

Ben shrugged. 'Most women I know need a bag this size just for their make-up.'

Katya found herself strangely irritated by his apparent knowledge of women and their luggage. 'I am not most women.'

Amen to that. Ben shut the lid down and gave the metal an affectionate tap. He glanced up to see her staring at the vehicle. 'What?' he asked warily.

She shrugged. 'I thought you'd drive a Ferrari or a Lamborghini.'

He smiled. 'Disappointed?'

'No. Surprised.'

Of course. Katya was truly the only woman he'd ever known who had been completely unimpressed with his title or his status. In fact, it had been obvious right from the start that she had resented his wealth. Had judged him harshly on the playboy image he projected through her jaded working-class eyes.

And the truth was, he *had* owned his share of status symbols, including a very sleek red Ferrari, but that had been in another life. Back when an indulgent, lavish lifestyle had been all he had known. But a lot of water had flowed under the bridge since then. And it bothered him that she found him wanting because of his bank account.

'Maybe you don't know me as well as you think,' he said, walking towards her and opening her door.

Katya raised an eyebrow. His entire time at MedSurg he'd been the epitome of a rich, spoiled playboy. The only time she had seen anything different had been the night they had made love. The night he'd received word of his brother's death.

That night she had seen a vulnerability, a glimpse of the man beneath the façade. All his layers had been stripped away by the shocking news and he'd been raw, totally open. The playboy had gone and the man had emerged. And she'd given him her virginity without a second thought. And that was the man she needed to be the father of her child.

'Maybe I don't,' she conceded.

Ben felt her warm breath on his cheek and was surprised by her concession. This was not the Katya he remembered. The sassy Katya. The Katya who gave him a hard time. The Katya who didn't give him an inch. But he had seen this Katya once before. The night she had offered him comfort and solace.

They were close now and visions of that night swamped him. He could smell her familiar scent. Cinnamon, just as he remembered, and he had a sudden urge to see if she would taste as he remembered, too. Her open-necked shirt afforded him a view of pale skin and prominent collar-bone and he suddenly wanted to lean in and nuzzle along the hard ridge and the hollow above.

Katya looked into his slumberous brown eyes and could see the passion flaring to life in their smouldering depths. Read exactly what he was thinking. God knew, she was thinking it herself. She could feel herself sway, hear her breath roughen, hear his follow suit.

A horn blared behind them, echoing around the cold cement corners of the car park, and they both froze. Katya's heart hammered as she pulled herself back from the brink. She was not here to pick up where they left off! She remembered how offhand he'd been the morning after, how confused she'd been by his casual job offer, like he'd just thrown money on her bedside table, and her determination to act like it hadn't been a big deal. She struggled to find that miraculous act again now.

'How long will it take to get to Ravello?' she asked as she slipped into the passenger seat on shaky legs.

'We are staying in Positano tonight,' he said when he joined her, 'in my mother's villa.'

He buckled up, noticing her body, which she'd been holding quite erect anyway, as if the luxury of the leather seats would taint her working-class skin, stiffen further.

'This was not part of the plan,' she said.

'My mother wishes to welcome you to Italy. She is preparing a feast in your honour. Relax,' he teased, and reached across to squeeze her denim-clad knee.

Katya glared at him and then at his hand, picked it up off her knee and put it back on the gear lever. 'That is not necessary.'

'My mother insists.' He shrugged. 'She will be very disappointed if we don't stop. We will go to Ravello in the morning. It is only half an hour, depending on traffic.'

He saw the grim set to her mouth and knew from experience she was itching to say more. He'd seen that glitter in her eyes before and had been the recipient of the caustic dialogue that usually followed. But he could also tell that she didn't want to offend his mother.

'Your mother knows we are work colleagues only, *da*? I trust we will have separate rooms?'

Ben couldn't help himself, he roared with laughter. His

mother was an old-fashioned woman, had raised them with traditional values. She thought premarital sex was a sin. 'You have nothing to fear there, Katya.'

'Good,' said Katya, and turned to gaze out of her window.

Ben concentrated on his driving, navigating his way out of Rome easily. He had spent a lot of his years in the capital and knew it well. The Medici family had residences in Rome and Florence and he had split his formative years between the two.

He took the *autostrada* exit to Naples. His family had always wintered on the Amalfi coast, his mother preferring the gentler climate of southern Italy, and the Positano villa had been her permanent home for five years now. For many years it had been his favourite place in all of Italy but too much had happened there and when he had left a decade ago he had sworn to never return. But the Lucia Clinic was there. His duty was there.

He glanced at Katya's profile. She appeared to be engrossed in the scenery and he took the opportunity to study her. She was dressed casually in hipster jeans. They were snug-fitting rather than tight, emphasising her slender thighs. Her white, short-sleeved shirt looked cool, the top few buttons undone, revealing a hint of cleavage.

Funny…he'd seen her almost every day for a year and yet had rarely seen her in civvies. In his mind, when he pictured her, which he did a little too often for his own sanity, it was as she'd been that last night. Gloriously naked, her body slick with sweat, her blue eyes wide and dazed with passion. He remembered the bite of her nails into his buttocks, the nip of her teeth into his shoulder, the gasps of pleasure from her mouth.

He dragged himself back from the fantasy with difficulty. Despite the evidence of his eyes, he couldn't quite believe that she was actually sitting here beside him.

To say he'd been surprised to take her call a few weeks ago was an understatement. After the way they'd parted, the way he'd acted after such an amazing night, it had hardly been his brightest moment.

Is that job offer still open? she had asked. And he had been so delighted to hear her accented English, so relieved that she was still talking to him after his morning-after bungle, that he'd forgotten what a shrew she could be and had said, *Of course.* In honesty, he'd missed her. Missed her frankness. Her cute accent. Her aloofness. She was the only woman he'd ever met who could turn him on through pure indifference.

In typical Katya fashion, she hadn't gone into detail about her reasons on the phone. She hadn't explained why she was now doing the very thing she'd told him she wouldn't. *I'd rather drink bad vodka,* that's what she'd told him that last morning. She had just lectured him about what her coming to Italy did and didn't mean. A work thing, she had said. No taking up where they had left off.

So why had she changed her mind? He had to admit to being a little more than curious. Perhaps she needed the money for some reason? The Lucia Clinic certainly paid its staff well. MedSurg, on the other hand, the charitable organisation they had both been employed by, while incredible to work for, did not.

But, then, no one joined its ranks to get rich. MedSurg involved a higher ideal. And Katya had been committed to staying on with them—for ever, she had said that awful morning. So something had come up to change her mind.

Wanting to change direction, she had told him on the phone. But he knew that was a lie. What were the words she had used when she'd first realised his family owned the world-renowned Clinic? *A place where rich vain people desper-*

ately trying to hold onto their youth were pandered to. Or words to that effect anyway. He smiled to himself. Would she tell him if he asked?

'Shouldn't you be watching the road?' Katya said, turning away from the window to pierce him with a disapproving glare.

Hmm. Maybe not.

Not even as the dense housing of Rome fell away and Italian countryside surrounded them could Katya ignore the weight of his stare. She'd been hyper-aware of him the minute she had spotted him, half-hidden behind the largest bouquet she had ever seen. She had hoped that their time apart would have put her attraction into perspective but, if anything, it seemed to be stronger.

It was the clothes, she decided. Although he filled out a pair of scrubs magnificently, it was nothing to how he looked dressed as Italian nobility. Everything about him screamed money. The cut of his trousers. The way the fabric of his shirt draped across the breadth of his shoulders and moulded to his chest, emphasising his six-foot-plus frame. The soft leather of his expensive shoes.

Who had said clothes maketh the man? Whoever it had been—they'd been right. In scrubs she'd been able to make believe he was just Ben. Gorgeous, flirtatious, persistent, annoying Ben. Ben the surgeon. That Ben had been relatively easy to ignore.

But in his civvies he looked…regal. Aristocratic. Like Count Benedetto Medici. Rich as sin. Hotshot plastic surgeon. And…the father of her baby. Katya knew she would find this Ben far from easy to dismiss.

Knew she couldn't afford to. Knew she had to get to know him. Get behind the façade, behind the clothes. Find the man she'd made love to three months ago, if indeed he actually existed, or whether he'd just been a temporary aberration in an extraordinary set of circumstances.

A car cut in front of them and then surged forward, swaying all over the *autostrada*, the white lines completely ignored.

Katya swore in Russian, clutching the dashboard, her heart racing at their near miss. 'Idiot,' she repeated in English at the car disappearing fast into the distance. 'Did you see that?' she asked, turning to him.

Ben chuckled. 'You will have a hoarse voice by the end of the day if you yell at everyone who does that. We Italians drive as we live. Passionately.'

'Bloody dangerously,' Katya muttered, trying not to think about the passionate Italian in Ben.

Ben had been right and the next two hours Katya clung to the edge of her seat as his powerful Alfa ate up the miles. 'Do you need to go so fast?' she asked him as she glanced at his speedometer and noticed he was going 140.

He smiled at her. 'This is not fast,' he said. As if to emphasise his point, three cars swerved around them and sprinted ahead, leaving the sporty car eating their fumes.

'Mad,' she said, shaking her head.

'This is nothing.' He winked. 'Wait till we get to the coast road.'

Katya wouldn't have believed that the experience could get any more terrifying, but she was wrong. The coast road was exactly as Ben had warned. A sheer white-knuckled adrenaline rush. The scenery was breathtaking on a sunny autumn afternoon—the craggy cliffs towering above them on one side and the sparkling blue Mediterranean on the other—but it was impossible to properly admire the majesty from behind her hands.

Speed was no longer an issue, too many cars made it impossible to get above forty. Now it was just sheer bloody-minded insanity. Cars and mopeds and trucks and tourist buses all vied for room on the narrow twisting roads that clung to the cliff face and even tunnelled through in places.

Cars were parked crazily on either side and sometimes both sides of the road, crammed into any remotely accessible space, narrowing the available room considerably. Katya covered her eyes as Ben manoeuvred his car through and around the general mayhem.

'It's a beautiful sunny Sunday. Italians always head for the beach,' he told her as he skilfully worked the gear lever.

She marvelled at how unruffled he appeared when her pulse was hammering madly in her neck. Mopeds darted around him like schools of fish, vehicles overtook them on blind corners and horns blared constantly. Some drivers even decided to pull up in the middle of the road and chat with pedestrians they apparently knew.

She had never seen such chaos in all her life. They traversed the narrow streets of villages, stopping for wandering dogs and groups of chatting locals. They passed dozens and dozens of restaurants and hotels lining the route, all decorated with gorgeous splashes of vibrant bougainvillea.

They passed several roadside vendors selling fruit from small trucks and even passed one with a raised metal frame upon which dozens and dozens of red chillies had been strung up, hanging in colourful plump bunches.

'Ben!' she yelled, pointing at an oncoming bus directly in their path as she clutched his thigh and shut her eyes.

Ben laughed and took the necessary evasive action. 'It's OK now, you can open your eyes,' he teased.

'Oh, God, how much longer?' she asked, still holding his

leg, the bulk strangely reassuring. It had taken them an hour
to travel a handful of kilometres.

'Not long.' He grinned down at her.

Katya found his smile contagious and the confidence in his
brown eyes soothing. She had seen that look, the calm, quietly
confident look, many times in his operating theatre. And she
needed that right now because the terrifying ride had wider
implications. There were three people in this car and the
thought of having an accident—the baby getting hurt—was
too much to bear.

She smiled back at him, pleased that on a scenic cliff road
on the Amalfi coast she was with someone who could handle
the perils of the journey. She became aware of her hand resting
on his thigh and felt heat creep into her face.

'Sorry,' she said, withdrawing her hand.

'Don't be,' he said, returning his attention to the road. 'It
felt good.'

Katya swallowed, her hand still warm from the bulky
muscle. Yes, it had. *Precisely why she shouldn't have done it.*

'Here it is,' he said a few minutes later, and turned off the coast
road onto the Via Pasitea, the main thoroughfare that meandered
down through the maze of cliff-face villas of Positano.

Katya breathed easier now the crazy pace and chaos had
settled. They were still being overtaken by the odd moped but
she didn't feel as if she was about to die. She even got to appreciate the scenery. It was late afternoon by now and the
fading sunlight reflected off the colourful façades of the buildings that lined the road and the cliff faces in every direction.

Yellow, pink, white, terracotta. Flowering bougainvillea
crept over walls and hung off trellises everywhere. Every
home, restaurant and hotel was decorated with flower boxes
ablaze with beautiful colourful blooms. The Mediterranean

sparkled in the distance. Positano dazzled the eye and Katya was instantly charmed.

Ben waved at people as he passed. They called out to him and he smiled and greeted them by name. He seemed to know everyone.

'A popular man,' she mused.

'My family has had a home here for many generations.' He shrugged.

Katya turned back to the window, keeping her eyes firmly trained on the scenery. How would that be? To have grown up here? For the baby to grow up here? She thought back to her dreary upbringing in Moscow. State housing, sketchy services, going hungry on too many nights, going cold even more and a pervading climate of fear that even as a child she had been aware of. No neighbours greeting you as a long-lost friend—just keep your head down and stay the hell out of trouble. She wanted more than that for this baby.

'Here we are,' he said, slowing the vehicle.

Katya could just make out a whitewashed villa through the mesh wire of a very high fence. Ben removed a remote control from the centre console and a heavy-duty security gate swung open. He drove into the narrow space, just big enough for two small cars, and turned the engine off.

'Welcome to Positano.'

Katya looked over at the imposing villa. Inside the fence it looked even grander, dominating the cliff face perched over the sea below. Its grandeur scared the hell out of her. She suddenly felt like Cinderella at the ball and hoped she didn't trip or say something stupid or eat with the wrong utensil.

She pictured Ben's mother, a plump old lady with a mole on her chin and a twinkle in her eye, slaving over a hot oven for her. For her. Cooking a feast, Ben had said. The last thing she wanted to do was show how very little breeding she had. Not because she cared necessarily but, hey, a girl had her pride.

She climbed out of the car and allowed Ben to get her case for her then lead her to the front door. The side wall that faced them was stark white, two rows of arched windows breaking up the line of the house. Terracotta window boxes overflowed with red geraniums.

They walked up a short flight of stone steps. Pretty tiles inlaid along the tread of each stair were beautifully decorative. A large wooden door was an impressive barrier to the outside world.

Ben inserted his key into the lock and pushed the heavy door open, gesturing for Katya to precede him. She stepped in nervously, the white walls, towering ceilings and large blue floor tiles, the exact tone of the sea, dazzling to the eye.

'Mamma,' he called.

He strode through the house and Katya followed close behind, awed by the expensive-looking furniture, rugs and artwork that decorated the Medici villa. She had the urge to huddle into the broad strength of his back, feeling a bit like Alice in Wonderland. It was only her pride that kept her frame erect and her hands firmly by her sides.

They entered the kitchen, which smelt amazing. A blend of garlic, basil and onions tickled Katya's nose and emphasised how long it had been since she had eaten.

'Benedetto? Benedetto?'

One of the most elegant-looking women Katya had ever seen entered the room from stairs to their right. She was tall and regal, her silver hair swept back into a glamorous chignon. So much for round and soft with a mole on her chin! She threw her arms in the air and broke into enthusiastic Italian as she embraced her son.

Katya stood back and watched their easy affection. She felt a pang of envy as his mother grabbed his cheeks and planted an enthusiastic kiss on each. Their closeness was a stark contrast to the strained relationship she shared with her own mother and Katya felt even more out of her depth.

The similarities between the two were striking. He had his mother's high cheekbones and her strong patrician nose. And as the older woman opened her eyes and smiled at her, Katya realised that this would be her baby's grandmother. There was so much love in this room, in this homey Italian kitchen, that Katya felt tears well in her eyes. She blinked them away quickly but not before she saw a faint narrowing of the older woman's eyes. Ben's mother had seen her tears.

'Mamma, this is Katya Petrova,' Ben said, pulling out of his mother's embrace. 'Katya, this is my mother, Contessa Lucia Medici.'

Katya held out her hand tentatively, not sure how to greet a contessa. 'It's a pleasure to meet you, Contessa,' Katya said.

The contessa smiled and came forward, her arm outstretched, too, firing rapid Italian.

'English, Mamma,' Ben broke in, reminding her gently.

'Of course, I'm sorry.' The contessa smiled at Katya, slipping easily into near perfect English. 'Forgive my manners. Please, call me Lucia.'

The contessa swept Katya into a hug as enthusiastic as the one she'd given to her own flesh and blood. Katya felt awkward in her embrace, completely unused to displays of motherly affection. But the contessa's eyes were kind and again she felt absurdly close to tears.

'Shall we adjourn outdoors?' Lucia suggested as she pulled away. 'Benedetto.' She turned to her son. 'Bring the wine,' she commanded.

Katya followed Lucia down the stairs from where she'd entered the kitchen earlier. It led to a magnificent terrace with one-hundred-and-eighty-degree uninterrupted views of the Mediterranean below and the majestic craggy coastline in both directions.

There was a round outdoor table with a striking ceramic top. It had been hand-painted with a typical Mediterranean lemon-grove scene. A bowl of the bright yellow fruit sat in the middle of the table and Katya could smell their magnificent tartness.

Ben joined them, glasses clinking. He placed them on the table and poured them each a generous measure. Katya placed a hand over her glass. Ben raised his eyebrows.

'Wine gives me a headache,' she said, saying the first thing that popped in to her head.

Ben gave her a disbelieving look. *Since when?* 'This from a girl who could drink vodka for Russia.'

'Benedetto,' his mother scolded, 'don't be rude. Run up and get some water.'

'Yes, Benedetto,' Katya teased, unable to resist. 'Run along.'

Too late Katya realised that Lucia might disapprove of her informality. What if she thought that Ben should be addressed as befitting a man of his stature? But the contessa clapped her hands gleefully and her eyes twinkled with delight. Katya breathed a sigh of relief.

Calling him by his title would be plain weird, given the things they had been through. The times they had stood side by side, their hands inside some stranger's body, locked in a battle for their life. Or the time they had sought solace in each other's bodies. Some relationships transcended titles and if their work relationship hadn't cut it then their intimate joining certainly had.

Ben chuckled and left to do his mother's bidding. He returned quickly with a bottle of sparkling water and poured some into Katya's glass. He sat in the chair beside her and she was instantly conscious of his potent male heat.

'To bossy Russian nurses,' Ben said, raising his glass.

'Benedetto!' Lucia gasped.

Katya saw the twinkle in his eye and the perfect upward curve of his beautiful full lips. 'To flashy Italian counts,' she parried.

Lucia laughed and raised her glass. 'Touché.'

They drank their drinks and ate bruschetta as the sun set and the lights of Positano, spread below them, gradually twinkled on one by one. Katya found herself relaxing in the pleasant company, with the stunning scenery a luxurious backdrop. Ben made her laugh and it was the most relaxed she'd been since she'd discovered her indiscretion had had consequences over a month ago.

Katya slipped easily into the banter she and Ben were known for in MedSurg circles. They entertained the contessa with stories from their travels and Lucia seemed to enjoy Katya's irreverent attitude towards her son.

After it was dark Lucia served up a delicious seafood pasta with a delicate creamy sauce. It was so good Katya even had a second helping. Sitting there, enjoying a balmy evening, under a canopy of stars, perched above the Med, Katya felt a real sense of family. It certainly wasn't something she was used to and…she liked it. Wanted the baby to grow up surrounded with the same sense of family.

Thinking about the baby brought her mission squarely back into focus. The evening had been a lovely distraction but she couldn't afford to lose sight of why she was here. Would Ben be a suitable father?

She watched him regaling his mother with a story and he was the charming playboy from MedSurg. And sitting amongst the trappings of his wealth, she knew that he could give their baby everything. But where was the Ben she'd seen that special night? The real man? The father-material man. Did he exist or was he just a figment of her overactive imagination?

Ben laughed and her skin broke out in goose bumps. It would be so easy to be distracted. Like she had been tonight. Seduced by the warmth and promise of a real family for her baby. She could even fool herself for a fleeting second that she could be part of it also.

Stop this! Katya stood abruptly. Ben and his mother looked at her enquiringly. 'I'm sorry, it's been a lovely night but would you mind if I went to bed, I'm very tired.'

'Of course not,' Lucia said. 'Come, I'll show you to your suite.'

Katya had to brush past Ben to join Lucia and she was super-aware of his heat and his scent as their bodies made the barest of contact. She bade him a brief goodnight, with a husky voice and trembling legs.

'Goodnight, *cara*,' Ben called after her.

She could see him in her peripheral vision, leaning lazily back against the chair, his long frame stretched out as graceful as a giant slumbering cat. She remembered vividly how great his length had felt pressed against her.

'This way,' Lucia said.

Katya didn't need any further encouragement. His wicked chuckle followed her all the way up the stairs.

'Here you are. Please, let me know if you need anything else,' Ben's mother said, opening the door to Katya's suite.

'Thank you, Lucia. You are most kind.'

The contessa shook her head. 'No. Thank you. I haven't

heard Benedetto laugh that much in many years. He is too serious these days.'

Katya watched Lucia withdraw and sat on the bed, staring after her. Ben? Serious? She'd only ever known Ben as he had been tonight. The life of the party. Flirty. Teasing. Except for that once when he'd been blindsided by grief and she'd seen an incredibly passionate side to him. Yet Lucia had hinted at another very different person again.

So who was the real Ben? The playboy? The serious son? Or the lover? That was her puzzle.

And would any of these Bens also be a good father?

CHAPTER TWO

Katya slept fitfully despite the luxury of her suite. She drew her knees up into her chest and hugged them to her. She was doing the right thing. She was. If nothing else, spending an evening with Ben and Lucia had proven that. The contessa was a warm, loving and supportive mother. She was affectionate. And also obviously worried about Ben. As far as motherly role models went, Katya figured you couldn't get any more exemplary.

But her? What role model did she have? What examples did she have to draw on, even subconsciously, to raise this baby right? None. From the age of eight she'd been the mother in their house. Had raised four siblings while her mother 'went out'. She knew enough about psychology to know that such cycles were too often repeated, and she was scared she'd fail. And she couldn't risk a child's life on it. And, frankly, she was twenty-seven and all mothered out.

Katya was grateful for daylight and pleased to hear movement downstairs. She showered and dressed quickly, zipping up her bag and carrying it with her, leaving it at the front door as she headed towards the kitchen.

Ben looked up from his coffee as she entered and gave her one of his killer smiles. '*Buongiorno*, Katya.'

Katya faltered a little. He looked very sexy this morning, sitting at the table like he was king of the castle. His hair was damp and his shirt was open at the throat, giving her a peek of the tanned column of his neck and a hint of chest hair. His brown eyes glowed warm and rich and tempting.

'You don't look like you slept very well.'

This man was too damn perceptive by half. 'Well, that's because I kept expecting to turn back into a pumpkin.'

Ben threw his head back and laughed. 'You think this is a fairytale?' He pushed a plate of sweet pastries her way and poured her a shot of espresso.

No. Fairytales had happy endings and Katya knew that for her there would be no happily-ever-after. But if she could secure one for her baby then she could rest easy knowing she had given it the best chance in life.

'I think you live a pretty charmed life,' said Katya, sitting and biting gratefully into a fruit-filled croissant with a sticky glaze.

Ben paused, his cup halfway to his mouth. He bit his lip to prevent a derisive snort from escaping his throat. He'd stopped feeling charmed a long time ago. About the time his older brother had stolen his fiancé. Katya's assumptions about his life goaded him to respond. If that was the way she still thought of him after their night together then so be it.

'Is there something wrong with that, Katya?'

Ben's voice was soft and silky, the hint of flint in it scraping seductively over her skin. Katya paused in mid-chew. Her breath caught in her chest at the intensity of his gaze. He seemed to be searching her soul, looking for the answer he wanted. She felt her nipples bead against the lacy fabric of her bra at the frank hunger in his eyes.

She shrugged. 'If you consider living in the lap of luxury

and pandering to the hedonistic lifestyle of the rich and famous at your clinic a worthwhile way to spend your time then who am I to say?'

Ben bit back the urge to set her straight. She could judge him at her own peril. 'Oh, come, now, Katya, don't tell me you could turn your back on all this? In fact, I could show you a really good time while you're here. Are you sure you don't want to pick up where we left off?'

Katya wasn't sure where this conversation was heading or even what it was really about any more. There was a dangerous glitter to his eyes. Gone was the teasing, flirty Ben. He looked every inch the aristocrat. A little ruthless and very virile. She didn't know this man at all.

She swallowed, his words seductive despite their cold edge. 'Strictly business, Ben. I meant what I said.' She forced her voice to be firm despite the quaking inside.

'Are you sure, *cara*?' he purred. 'We were good.'

Ben's soft, deep voice held her captivated. It had been good. Very, very good. 'It was a mistake,' she said, dismayed to hear the words coming out all husky.

Ben was surprised that her barb stung. It had been the only thing that had meant anything to him in the last decade. He held her gaze. 'It could be fun, Katya Petrova.'

She could feel her eyes widen at the promise in his words. She believed him. Now, that would be a first. Since when had life been just pure fun?

Stop this, Katya. Only the baby mattered now. 'I'm not the fun type,' she said emphatically, brushing the flaky crumbs of pastry from her hand, swallowing her espresso in one hit and standing. 'Shouldn't we be going?'

Ben chuckled, shrugging off the darkness she had aroused in him. She was right—no one who knew her would describe

Katya as fun. Blunt. Efficient. Sharp-witted. Quick-tongued.
A sense of humour that bordered on the sarcastic. But fun? No.

'Come on, then. If we leave now, we should be in Ravello
in plenty of time to show you around before the first case.'

She followed him to the front door. 'Shouldn't we say
goodbye to your mother?'

'Mamma doesn't rise before ten,' he said, picking up
Katya's case.

Katya stared after him, the denim of his jeans clinging to
the contours of his bottom perfectly. *It could be fun*, whispered
insidiously through her head as she pulled the door closed
behind her.

Ben smiled to himself as he glanced down and noticed Katya's
hands gripping the edge of her seat, her knuckles white.
'Relax,' he teased.

'Easy for you to say.'

'This is nothing,' he said, changing gear as the traffic
slowed a little on the outskirts of Amalfi. 'Wait till we start
to climb higher.'

'Goody, goody gumdrops,' Katya said, quoting a favoured
expression of Dr Guillaume Remy, a colleague they had
worked with at MedSurg.

Ben laughed at the slang pronounced in sexily accented
English. 'How are Guillaume and Harriet?' he asked. 'Are
they pregnant yet?'

Katya nodded, feeling her spirits lift. 'Their second cycle
of IVF worked. Their baby is due in the New Year,' she said,
remembering how close Harriet and Gill had come to divorc-
ing over the baby issue. And now here she was—also with a
baby quandary.

At least she'd be able to return to MedSurg after the baby.

Her colleagues there were the closest thing she'd ever had to a real family and it would be good to get straight back into the all-consuming work. To forget that she'd left her baby with Ben.

'That's great,' said Ben. He remembered how much he had enjoyed his time with the aid organisation and how good Gill had been with him. Performing surgery in the middle of a war zone had been a steep learning curve but he had flourished and learnt a lot.

Leaving had been hard, especially with the tempting presence of one Katya Petrova, and had his hand not been forced by his brother's death, Ben would still be working for them. But he'd returned home, despite his decade-old vow not to, to a job he despised and a life he hadn't wanted. He could feel the familiar tension creep into his neck muscles and along his jaw and he tightened his grip on the steering wheel.

The road came back down to sea level and he glanced over to the harbour on his right and saw his gleaming white boat, *The Mermaid*, bobbing in the calm water. He looked at her clean sleek lines and felt himself relax again.

'My boat,' he said to Katya and pointed. 'I'll take you out in it this weekend.'

'Don't bother. I get seasick,' she said bluntly.

Ben found her determination to keep things 'strictly business' amusing and laughed as he changed gear. He looked at her face, her cute button nose, her beautiful blue eyes, her soft mouth with its tempting full lips, high cheekbones and blonde pixie cut that feathered around her face. She was sassy and sexy and had the mouth of a shrew and, God help him, he wanted her!

He remembered what else her mouth could do when it wasn't busy putting him in his place. He remembered how she had kissed him with an intensity and reckless abandon that had stunned him and knew behind her no-nonsense façade lurked a very passionate woman.

He thought back to past relationships. How easy they'd been. How meaningless. He'd filled his life with pretty women since Bianca's betrayal, trying to exorcise his demons. Women who had been eager and willing. Who'd enjoyed the favours of a rich, generous playboy. But not one of them had got beneath his skin like this unimpressed, practical Russian nurse. What the hell would it take to impress her? And why the hell did it matter so much?

Katya shut her eyes as the mountain road narrowed even further than the coast road. It seemed like nothing more than a goat track in places. But every time her lids closed all she saw was his damn boat. Big and white and expensive. The type of boat she saw in magazines where royalty lounged on sundecks. She had half expected to see a movie star emerging from one of the galleys of the rows and rows of luxurious vessels.

She should be happy. Yet another confirmation that he could provide for their baby so much better than her. But strangely his wealth, which had always bothered her, seemed to bother her twice as much. His boat was a big flashy status symbol—like an aquatic Ferrari. And he'd asked her to join him. How many other women had he had on that boat? How many women would he parade in front of their child?

She'd grown up seeing a procession of partners through her mother's life. And how screwed up was she today? Her mother had been seduced into neglecting her children and Katya had been wise in the ways of the world way before her time. Is that what Ben would do? Neglect their child in favour of his lifestyle? He was a thirty-five-year-old playboy bachelor. An Italian count. Aristocracy, for God's sake. Was it even possible to give that lifestyle away?

They made it to Ravello by quarter past eight and Ben drove the Alfa through an arch in a vine-covered wall. They entered a large cobblestoned courtyard dominated in the centre by a spectacular fountain. There was ample room for several cars and Ben angled his into a reserved space.

'Welcome to the Lucia Clinic,' he said. 'Otherwise known as the palace for hedonistic rich people.'

Katya turned and gave him a withering smile. 'If you can't stand the heat, Count, get out of the kitchen.' And she opened the door and climbed out, his laughter following her.

The building was impressive. It was a U-shaped structure built around the courtyard. The wall they had just driven through towered behind her as high as the other buildings and gave the courtyard and the clinic a private feel, protecting it from view. The rendered walls were painted a pale orange, their aged, weather-beaten appearance giving the clinic a timeless quality.

Ben opened the boot and removed their bags. 'The main wing, in front of you,' he said, indicating the longest section of the clinic, 'is the patients' suites. We have twenty beds. Twelve suites and four twin share rooms. The west wing holds the operating theatres and X-ray facilities, the east wing is the kitchens and staff accommodation.'

'You have a lot of staff that live on site?' she asked following him as he moved towards the entrance.

'There are twenty rooms, but only half are used permanently as most of our staff live locally and commute. The others are used casually. I bunk down here during the week and, of course, one of these rooms will be yours.'

Katya could feel his gaze on her and refused to look at him. The mere thought of him sleeping nearby did funny things to her breathing. It had been the same during their time at

MedSurg. Communal staff facilities had seen to it that too often he had been the last person she had seen before going to bed and the first one she'd seen on waking.

'Come on, I'll introduce you around. Everyone is very friendly here and most speak English.'

Katya followed him through the magnificent arched entrance and almost gasped at the cool elegance of the reception area. It was luxurious. No expense had been spared, from the artwork on the walls to the marble on the floor to the crystal chandelier hanging above the sweeping stone staircase dominating the entrance hall.

Ben showed her to her quarters first. Katya put her bag on the bed as Ben stood in the hallway. She looked around at cool decorative tiles underfoot and the mirror edged with pretty ceramic tiles inlaid into an arched recess in the wall. It was beautiful but she was more conscious of him breathing and his bulky presence against the doorjamb and what had happened last time he had stood in her doorway. She wondered where he slept and then halted her thoughts. His quarters were of no concern to her.

'Come,' Ben said, 'meet some of the staff.'

Katya didn't have to be asked twice.

Ben introduced her to so many people her head spun and she knew it would take her a few days to remember everyone. He gave her a tour of all the medical facilities, including the two operating rooms.

'Is this the theatre list?' she asked, looking at the typed list stuck to Theatre Two's main door.

He nodded. 'For this theatre, yes.'

Katya scanned the scheduled operations, thankful to find it was written in Italian and English. Abdominoplasty. Rhinoplasty. Augmentation mamoplasty. She felt her heart sink. Tummy tuck. Nose job. Boob job.

She had known the Lucia Clinic was an exclusive plastic surgery clinic but seeing it in reality hammered it home. It was hard to believe that someone who had worked in war zones could ever consider pandering to such vanity worthwhile.

Ben could easily read the distaste on her face. He remembered his first day at the clinic, shaking his head in disbelief, too. 'Would you like to see the gardens?' he asked.

'Sure,' Katya said vaguely.

They wandered back through the building, Katya dazed from the opulence all around her. No expense had been spared anywhere. From the fittings to the surgical equipment, everything was high quality, top notch, the best that money could buy. It was a little sickening, actually. How many people could MedSurg and aid organisations like it help if they had this sort of money at their disposal?

Ben took her through one of the private suites that was empty and pushed open the doors onto a small balcony. Katya's breath caught in her throat as the magnificence of the view hit her. The grounds below had been terraced down the side of the hill and beautiful gardens adorned the rocky slope. Fountains and water features and lush greenery punctuated by colourful blooms, dazzled the eye.

And beyond the grounds was the endless blue of the Mediterranean. It sparkled in the mid-September sunshine like a beautiful priceless sapphire. The craggy cliffs dominating the coastline were breathtaking in their enormity, towering high into the sky and tumbling in weathered splendour to plunge to the sea.

Katya looked either side of her. Each suite had its own balcony and she was hard pressed to think of a more beautiful place to recover from surgery. It was a stark contrast to her

MedSurg job where patients too often recovered in cramped, less than ideal conditions.

'This villa is centuries old, as are many of the buildings around here,' said Ben. 'Ravello is famous for its villas and their beautiful gardens. Many Hollywood films were filmed here back in the early nineteen hundreds and there are regular chamber music concerts held throughout the village during the year.'

'It's amazing,' she said, the sheer beauty holding her in awe, the decadence overwhelming.

Ben heard a hesitant note in her voice. 'You don't sound so sure,' he said.

'No, it's…it's…wow.'

'Sounds like there's a "but" there.' He smiled. He knew exactly what she was thinking.

Katya shrugged. Her poor-as-dirt background and some of the horrors she had seen working with MedSurg made it difficult to reconcile the indulgences of the affluent. 'I was just thinking how different it is from some of the places I've been with MedSurg.'

He nodded. 'That it is.'

Katya blinked at his understatement. It seemed so flippant when she knew, as did he, there were people out there who couldn't get proper health care at all.

'Don't you think all this is a little obscene?' She felt nauseated suddenly by it all and wondered if she could truly let her baby be brought up by someone who couldn't see how indulgent it was.

Sure, she wanted her baby to be provided for, to have the stuff she never had, but she also wanted it to have a sense of humanity. She had thought as Ben had worked for MedSurg that he had that kind of compassion, but if he could come back to this and not feel tainted by the excess then maybe she was wrong.

Ben could feel his ire beginning to rise again. She was doing it again. Judging him. It hadn't mattered so much at MedSurg, his wealth had irritated her and he had exploited that role to the hilt because she had looked so cute when she'd been mad. But things had changed since then and her assumptions annoyed him. 'You think it's wrong? You don't approve of vanity?'

Katya schooled her features. Obviously she was letting her distaste show. 'I think all the bad stuff happening in the world is more important than whether your nose is too big or your tummy too fat.' She tried to keep the bluntness out of her voice but on this subject her passion ran deep.

Ben couldn't agree more. 'And yet you rang and asked me for a job. You knew what we do here. Why did you come if it was going to offend your sensibilities?'

His question caught her unawares. She wasn't ready to open up yet. Oh, God, how could she say, *Because I'm having your baby and I need to check out if you're worthy of raising it because I'm certainly not.*

'I told you, I want to change direction.'

'You? Leave MedSurg? I don't believe it.'

Neither did she! And as soon as this was all over, she was heading straight back to a workplace with some backbone. But for now, for the sake of her baby, she needed to suffer the whims of the wealthy.

'If you didn't want me to come you shouldn't have offered me a job.' Katya knew from long experience that the best defence was offence. 'But, then, you weren't really serious, were you? We both knew it was just a throw-away line the morning after.'

Ben felt her accusation hit him square in the solar plexus. His guilt from that morning came flooding back. She was right. He had handled the whole thing very badly. He had known it back then but his apology had been stalled by her scathing reaction to his job offer.

She was standing with her back to him, her hands gripping the railing. She reminded him of how she'd been that morning. Erect. Distant. He wanted to touch her but couldn't bear to see her shrink from his touch like she had that day also. 'About that morning…' he said.

Katya gripped the railing harder and held her breath. She had spent months trying to forget the incident, she didn't want to rehash it now, especially not when their child was already a constant reminder.

'Benedetto!'

Both Ben and Katya startled at the unexpected interruption and turned to see Gabriella, one of the nurses she had met earlier, come bustling in, a child wearing a blue theatre cap on her hip.

Gabriella smiled at Katya. 'Lupi has been asking for you.'

Ben smiled at the little girl, her bilateral cleft lip making it impossible for her to smile back, but he could see the happiness shining in her eyes. 'Has she, now?' he growled and reached out to take the child from Gabriella who went eagerly. 'Well, now, little Lupi,' he said kissing her jet-black hair, 'you found me.'

Katya watched as the girl bounced up and down excitedly in Ben's arms. Katya guessed the child to be about three but she was obviously malnourished so she could well be older. But there was no mistaking the look of adoration in the girl's eyes.

Katya swallowed as Ben grinned down at her and Lupi snuggled her head into his chest. Where did Lupi fit in at the Lucia Clinic? Someone had been remiss in their care for her if her lip was only being repaired now. It didn't seem like something someone with money, with choices, would do. Her large almond-shaped eyes didn't look Italian either. Katya looked at Ben with confused eyes.

'Katya, this is Lupi,' Ben said. 'Lupi, this is Katya. She's going to help me with your operation today. We're going to give you your smile back.'

The little girl looked at her with solemn brown eyes and it took Katya a few moments to remember her manners. She smiled at the little girl. 'Hello, Lupi.'

'She doesn't understand English,' said Ben, rocking. 'Or Italian for that matter.'

'You're operating on her?'

Ben nodded. 'Lupi's is one of four operations I'm doing in Theatre One today for the Lucia Trust.'

Katya was still confused. 'The Lucia Trust?'

'A charitable organisation I founded on my return home. We perform operations on people, children mainly, with disfiguring conditions who don't have access to proper surgical intervention because of their circumstances.'

Katya found what he was saying hard to take in. But as the full implications sank in, she felt increasingly foolish. The things she had thought! The things she had said! And he hadn't corrected her. Just let her go on thinking the worst.

He chuckled. 'What's the matter, Katya? You're looking a little uneasy.'

His laugh was sexy as hell and it scraped along her nerves. He was rubbing his chin absently back and forth against Lupi's hair in time with his rocking. He looked very male and she felt her nipples peak despite her annoyance at him. 'You could have said something,' she said, her voice low, the note of accusation easy to detect.

He laughed again. 'And spoil your condemnation of me? Your problem, sweet Katya,' he said, tapping her on the nose, 'is that you are a reverse snob. You think everyone who has money isn't worthy. Is frivolous. You judge me because I'm wealthy and dismiss me as a rich playboy.'

A denial rose in her throat and died a quick death. It was true, she had. She did. But he had done nothing to dissuade her of her opinion. If anything he had nurtured it.

He leaned in close to her and said in a slow deep voice, 'Don't dismiss me, Katya.'

The words were like a caress and she swallowed hard. There was just something about his mouth, the way he stared at her from under half-closed lids, his eyelashes long and glorious. She could feel his slumberous gaze on her lips and could feel herself swaying closer before he pulled back and turned on his heel and exited, chatting to Lupi as he went.

Katya drew in a ragged breath and watched him walk away. She was too speechless to talk and too boneless to move so she stood and stared, trying to work out everything that had just transpired.

She wasn't sure who Ben was any more. She was so positive she'd had him pegged. With MedSurg he had been every bit the playboy count. Flirting and oozing sex appeal. Flashing his sexy smile and his diamond signet ring and managing to pull a packet of expensive chocolates or a tin of exclusive caviar out of thin air at the bleakest of times.

And yet this Ben was the opposite. He wasn't flashy or showy. He hadn't blown his own trumpet over the Lucia Trust and had cuddled Lupi to his chest like he had ten of his own children. She'd come to Italy to find out his suitability as a father. It was supposed to have been easy. But she was more confused than ever.

* * *

The theatre list got under way and right from the start Katya was aware of the differences between this and her MedSurg job. MedSurg dealt with major trauma. Big, ugly injuries. It was about saving lives, not delicate, intricate operations. It was fast, furious surgery. Patch 'em up and fly 'em out and start all over again. It was high-octane surgery.

This theatre was the exact opposite. There was no urgency, no sense of lives hanging in the balance, no adrenaline buzz. It was calm and ordered and relaxed, and Katya was surprised how nice that was for a change. She hadn't realised how much of an adrenaline junkie she'd become or how soothing a slower pace could be.

Maria, the nurse in charge of the operating suites, had put her on two days of scout nurse duty to ease her into the routine and familiarise her with the layout and had her down scrubbing from Wednesday onwards. Watching the preparations, Katya was surprised at how much she'd missed working. She'd been away from it now for a couple of months and she was itching to gown up again.

Ben winked at her over the top of his mask and she felt her skin flush beneath her mask, still embarrassed by her gaffe. So, now he felt superior to her, he was back to being flirty again? Well, at least she felt on firmer ground with this Ben. Flirty Ben she was used to. Serious, humanitarian, Lupi-cuddling Ben she wasn't.

'Do you want to have a closer look, Katya?'

Ben's words broke into her thoughts and she slowly met his gaze. *That's why I'm here, Ben—to get a closer look.*

'Katya?'

She blinked. 'Sure,' she said, ordering her legs to move. In fact, this operation had really piqued her interest. Not just because the little girl in question must have suffered so much with her disfiguring condition but because she was so relieved it wasn't someone voluntarily mutilating themselves, chasing some crazy beauty ideal.

She moved closer to the table opposite Ben, taking care to leave a little distance between her and the sterile drapes so she wouldn't contaminate them with any body contact. She wouldn't make herself popular if they had to redrape the patient.

'As you can see, Lupi's cleft is quite extensive,' Ben said, making his initial incision. 'She's lucky that her palate's not involved and that she only has a nasal deformity unilaterally on the left.'

'What's her story?' Katya asked.

'She comes from a remote village in her country that doesn't have access to health care. When she was born her mother and father thought she would die. When she didn't the village thought she was cursed. The villagers were too frightened to ostracise the family in case Lupi cursed them, too. But Lupi's mother has kept her hidden away in their dwelling for six years. The other children are very cruel.'

'Poor Lupi,' Katya said, a touch of anguish in her voice. She thought about how much Sophia, her own sister, had been through with her disfiguring injuries and how heartbroken she'd been whenever a kid from school had teased her. Katya's heart went out to this poor little girl. No wonder she seemed to be thriving with the attention she was getting here.

Ben flicked his gaze up from what he was doing. He'd heard the genuine distress in her comment. The little girl's plight had affected him, too. He couldn't imagine how awful it had been for her to be rejected by everyone around her and isolated from the normal life of a child.

At Lupi's age he and Mario had been inseparable, tearing around trying to outdo each other with more and more impressive deeds. He had been younger by a year but he'd never let that get between him and Mario and their hijinks. Poor Lupi had known none of that. She'd never been allowed to mix with other children.

'Indeed,' he said. 'She can't talk and has a very poor nutritional state because chewing and swallowing are so difficult with the bilateral cleft.'

Katya nodded. If Lupi had grown up somewhere with decent access to a good health-care system, she would probably have had several operations by now and had many specialties involved. Orthodontists, speech therapists, ENT surgeons, paediatricians, dieticians.

'Are you going to repair the nasal deformity in this operation as well?' Katya asked.

He nodded as he accepted his next instrument from the scrub nurse standing next to him. 'There are differing opinions on whether this should be done as a staged repair but Lupi's situation is very different,' he said. 'For a start, she's a lot older. Most children having this repair would be under a year old. And follow-up could be a problem. So I'll do both now. It may be that she'll need another operation in a few years' time as she grows and her facial structures mature but, as I say, follow-up could be a problem.'

Ben worked on the nasal defect, knowing he had to maintain symmetry and secure primary muscle union. He wanted to get the best outcome possible for Lupi, given everything she'd been through, but he was finding concentrating difficult with Katya standing a metre away.

He realised how much he'd missed being in the same theatre with her. It had only been a few months but he was looking forward to when she could scrub in with him in a few days. While she was close now, she could be closer and he wanted to be rubbing shoulders with her again.

Returning to Italy had put a very abrupt end to the 'thing' that had been happening between them. Oh, sure, Katya would have denied it but there had been a tension between them right from the beginning. He half suspected that was why she'd been so prickly, so feisty. Because deep down she'd also known something had been happening and it had scared her to death.

'Nearly done,' Ben said, asking for a suture.

Katya watched Ben's fingers as he operated, and allowed his deep husky tones to flow over her. He was concentrating, pulling the incised edges of the cleft together, preparing for closure. She studied his style and compared him to Gill Remy, the surgeon she had worked closely with at MedSurg.

Gill's fingers had been deft, his style understated and methodical. Ben's was different again. He was more flamboyant, his style entertaining. His movements were a little more exaggerated, his handiwork punctuated with an added flourish and touch of theatre.

It didn't affect his competency, she realised. It was more a reflection of his personality. Gill was a born surgeon, his skill and expertise defining him. Ben was a born count playing at being a surgeon. A rich man mixing it with the peasants and enjoying the freedom both worlds gave him. His style was…expressive, a bit like a conductor of a symphony orchestra, and Katya enjoyed watching him work.

The operation took an hour and Katya was amazed, as she always was, that time could pass so quickly when you were totally engrossed. Ben's handiwork was very impressive. The suture line dominating Lupi's now complete lip was obviously very prominent but Katya knew it would eventually fade to a ghostly white and the little girl that had been formerly shunned as a cursed child could now live a normal life.

And Ben had given that to her. For nothing. And if that wasn't true father material—then what the hell was?

CHAPTER THREE

ON FRIDAY morning, Katya finished breakfast a little earlier so she could stop by Lupi's room on her way to work. It was Lupi's last day and she wanted to pop in and say goodbye to the little girl who had won all of their hearts with her big brown eyes and beautiful new smile. Katya stopped abruptly at the door as she realised she'd been beaten to it.

Ben was speaking to her in Italian, their heads almost touching as they bent over a colouring book. Katya couldn't understand what was being said—hell, neither could Lupi—but the little girl giggled and beamed at Ben as he pulled funny faces while he coloured.

His rich deep voice traversed the distance between them and she almost sighed it sounded so good. Like the first coffee of the day, or a Sunday morning sleep-in or a crackling log fire in the middle of winter. She liked listening to him talk in his native tongue and she let her head relax against the doorjamb.

Lupi laughed and looked up at Ben with such trust in her eyes that Katya's heart skipped a beat. She knew in that moment that coming to Italy had been the right thing to do. That Ben was the perfect choice to raise their child. That if he could show this much compassion to a stranger, to a child he'd never even known until this week, his own child would be very lucky indeed.

It gave her a huge sense of relief, a sense of rightness, knowing that their child would look at him with the same measure of trust. Had she ever looked at her mother with such trust?

'You'd make a great father.'

Ben turned and saw Katya standing in the doorway. He looked back at Lupi, so defenceless, so trusting. He hadn't felt love for anyone or anything in a long time. Not a woman, not his country, not even his job. Not since Bianca and Mario. How could he give a child the love it deserved when he still felt so emotionally barren?

'No. I wouldn't.'

Katya felt a nudge of dread at the blunt rejection in his voice. 'You don't want to be a father someday?'

Ben returned to the colouring-in. Did he? Once upon a time he'd thought he and Bianca would have a tribe of kids. But he was older now, wiser. And still a little old-fashioned where children were concerned. It must be his mother's influence. His traditional upbringing.

He truly thought it was best that a man and a woman should be married before deciding to bring children into the world. That the parents should love each other and have made a binding commitment to be together for ever. Or at least he had anyway, before Mario and Bianca's actions had irreparably shaken his faith in love and marriage and family. He didn't know what the hell he believed any more, he just knew he wasn't ready for fatherhood.

'I'm too selfish,' he said dismissively.

Before coming to Italy, Katya would have agreed without hesitation. But looking at him now, sitting on a little girl's bed dressed in his scrubs, passing the time with her in the last few minutes before he had to start work, told her different.

'A selfish man would be enjoying an extra espresso or a few more minutes' sleep or relaxing over a newspaper,' Katya said quietly.

Ben stopped colouring and fixed her with a serious look. 'Don't read too much into this.'

He had to want to be a father. *He had to!* 'Sometimes we don't know what we're capable of until we try,' Katya said quietly, ignoring how much of a hypocrite that made her.

Ben put down the crayon he was using, turned back to Lupi and smiled. 'I'll be back later, little one,' he said, in English this time. Lupi smiled and waved as Ben eased himself off the bed and headed towards Katya.

He stopped in the doorway. He was close enough to smell her cinnamon scent. She was in her scrubs and the desire to see her out of them stormed through him. But talk of children dampened his ardour. Suddenly she'd made his life seem so bleak.

He placed his hand on the doorjamb above her head and leaned in, his mouth close to her ear. If he moved a fraction more he could pull the lobe into the wet cavern of his mouth, and fleetingly he was tempted. 'Children aren't something people should just *try, cara.* And my life is fine the way it is.' He pulled back a little and looked into her wide blue eyes.

Katya held his gaze, her heartbeat thundering in her ears. Fine? Just fine? Not happy, full, content? He didn't look fine. She could see a bleakness in his steady brown gaze. Here was the Ben she kept seeing glimpses of, the Ben that the contessa was worried about.

Ben could see Katya's keen gaze assessing him and he pushed away from her, not willing to share his deepest darkest thoughts with her. She was too damn astute and as he'd told her, his life was fine. Their arms brushed slightly as he passed her. *Fine, damn it!* If he could just stop thinking about her out of those damn scrubs!

Katya's stomach muscles contracted at the slight touch and she placed her hand protectively over her stomach as it looped the loop. So, he didn't want a baby? Well, neither did she. But whether he liked it or not, he *was* this baby's father. And he was a hell of a lot better equipped than she was to take care of it.

Katya inhaled swiftly as a sudden sharp pain flared in her chest. She ignored it, smiled and waved at Lupi then headed towards Theatre One. Some things in life were difficult. It didn't mean that they weren't right. She couldn't afford to think emotionally. She had to be practical. And luckily, thanks to her mother, Katya was a very practical person.

The morning cases got under way with Ben his usual jovial self again. She noticed he was always in high spirits while he operated and it was obvious that he thrived doing this kind of work. This morning they had a couple of children who had very bad burns contractures of their arms, making straightening them and their daily activities excessively difficult, limiting their independence.

One was a nine-year-old girl whose fingers on her burnt hand were being dragged into a claw shape due to severe flexion scar contractures, and the other was a four-year-old boy whose right arm was permanently bent up due to a contracture over his elbow joint.

They were brother and sister who had been involved in a tragic fire in their family dwelling that had also killed their mother. Both had had delayed and inadequate treatment of their burns, as so often happened in remote and poor communities. No burns protocols, no immediate grafting, no physio or splinting or pressure garments.

The Lucia Trust had been alerted to their cases through a charitable organisation in Africa and had flown them to Italy. It was Ben's job to debride the thickened scar tissue that was causing their problems and then cover the defects with a skin graft.

Katya could see he was totally in the zone, relishing the challenge, eager to make a difference to these children's lives. His excitement was palpable and the whole theatre was humming with anticipation.

Katya was excruciatingly aware of him today. It wasn't just his elevated mood but the memory of their earlier conversation, the way her heart beat had accelerated and her stomach had turned over at his closeness. She really needed some distance from him but scrubbing in with a surgeon always necessitated close contact and today was no different.

They both needed to see what they were doing, he to operate, she to anticipate his needs, and as much as she tried to distance herself it made very little difference to their proximity.

And despite her head telling her to keep it professional, focus on the job, her body had other ideas. When their arms clad in thick long-sleeved cotton gowns brushed together, it was if he had stroked her bare skin. When their gloved fingers touched as they exchanged instruments, it felt as if he had trailed them up her arm. When his low voice rumbled in her ear it felt as if he had feathered kisses down her neck.

Not even the music was a distraction. Ben liked to listen to classical music as he operated. Being Russian, she was quite partial to classical music herself, but it seemed weirdly intimate and she found herself pining for the dulcet tones of

Ella Fitzgerald who had serenaded them during her time with MedSurg, working with Gill Remy.

The CD that was playing today was Wagner. It was a poignant collection and she could feel her emotions see-saw with the rise and fall of the music. Wagner had been inspired by Ravello, Ben told her with pride, as he debrided scar tissue. The sexy timbre of his voice slid down her spine and ruined her concentration.

By the time Ben was satisfied with his work and the list came to an end she was eager to escape for a while. She needed to get as far away from him as was humanly possible. She'd come to her decision, there was no point buying into the attraction between them. All she had to do now was hang around until she'd had the baby and then get away—fast.

The list complete, Ben was just degowning when the wall phone rang. Being the closest, he picked it up.

'Lucia Clinic, Dr Medici speaking,' he said in Italian.

A woman replied. She was speaking in very broken, heavily accented English. 'I speak to Katya Petrova…please… I her…mama.'

Katya's mother? 'Of course,' he said switching to English. 'She is here. One moment.'

He looked up to see Katya just disappearing through the door. 'Katya,' he called after her.

She stopped and turned around. *What now?* She'd nearly escaped, damn it!

Ben held the phone out to her. 'It's for you. It's your mother.'

Oh, God! Had something happened to one of her siblings or was it just more of the usual? Katya covered the distance between the two of them quickly and practically snatched the phone from him.

'Mama?'

'*Da*,' her mother said.

'What's wrong?' Katya asked, slipping into her native tongue, gripping the phone, preparing for the worst.

'Katya,' her mother said reprovingly, 'can't I just ring and talk to my daughter without something being wrong?'

Since when had Olgah ever rung just to shoot the breeze with her firstborn? 'Everyone's OK, then?' Katya said. Her youngest sibling was now seventeen but that still didn't stop Katya fretting over them like a mother hen.

'*Da*, *da*,' Olgah said dismissively.

Katya breathed a sigh of relief and loosened her grip on the phone. She was conscious in her peripheral vision of Ben's blatant curiosity. He was sitting in the anesthetist's chair, pretending interest in a chart.

If there wasn't something wrong then Katya knew where this conversation was going to head, and she didn't want Ben to be privy to it. She turned slightly so she couldn't see him and leant heavily against the wall. She scuffed her feet against the floor, her head downcast, her free hand massaging her forehead.

'What do you want, Mama?' Katya asked, feeling herself tense.

'Katya! How can you speak to your mother like that?'

Katya ignored the indignation. 'How much, Mama?'

'I need a couple of thousand. I'm a little behind on the rent and I've just got the second notice from the electric company.'

The figure didn't even make Katya blink. Was it a new dress or a pair of shoes or a new man that had taken precedence over the rent and electricity? Katya sighed. 'Mama…'

'Please, Katya. It's expensive with four teenagers. And if you ever bothered to come home instead of tripping around the world, you'd know that.'

Katya gripped the telephone receiver and bit her tongue,

the unfairness of her mother's statement stinging. Like she'd been on a round-the-world trip! She'd been working her butt off in some of the world's hotspots so she could support her mother and four siblings. She knew how expensive it was, damn it. She'd been practically supporting the entire family since she'd started work.

'If it's too much for you maybe you can ask your rich count for a loan?'

'Mama!' Katya gasped.

Was her mother serious? She'd known the minute she'd told her mother that she knew a count and was going to Italy to work for him in the world-famous Lucia Clinic that she'd said the wrong thing. But her mother had been persistent in wanting to know why she was leaving MedSurg and a steady source of income and Katya certainly wasn't about to tell her about the baby.

And, just for once, she'd wanted for her mother to be impressed. Proud even. But, as usual, her mother didn't fail to disappoint her.

'Oh, don't be so shocked, Katya. You always were so high and mighty.'

'Well, somebody had to be, Mama.'

As soon as the words were out, Katya regretted them. Not because they were wrong but because she knew what was coming next. Katya held the phone and listened while her mother gave her the usual hard-luck story. How hard her life had been with five children and no man about the house. How she'd done the best she could with what she had. What an ungrateful daughter she was.

And then the real prize. 'You think you're better than me? Don't forget, if it wasn't for you, Katya, Sophia wouldn't be so horribly disfigured.'

No matter how many times she prepared herself for it, how many times she heard it, it still rocked her to the core. The angry little girl inside who had lost her childhood to her mother's reproductive irresponsibility clawed and begged and screamed to retaliate. To respond with righteous indignation. But the guilt, the guilt her mother knew how to manipulate so well, paralysed the words, froze them in her throat, every time.

She looked up and saw Ben watching her. 'I'll send the money, Mama,' Katya said, her voice shaky, her hands trembling as she cast her eyes downwards again.

'Good girl.'

No 'thank you'. No apologies for asking or lamenting her incompetence with money.

'You know, Katya,' Olgah continued, 'if you played your cards right, were nice to your boss, he might… I know from the magazines he's a terrible playboy but he might like a nice little Russian girl. We'd never have to worry about money again.'

Olgah was so matter-of-fact that Katya felt physically ill. She realised for the first time, as an emotion so vile injected its poison through her body, that she hated her mother. There had been plenty of times growing up—home alone, trying to raise her four siblings while her mother 'went out'—when she had felt rage and fury and frustration towards her.

But this? Suggesting first that she go to Ben for money and then that she ingratiate herself to ensure a lifetime of financial security for her family? This was truly corrupt, even for her mother. It became imperative to Katya right then and there that her mother never find out that the baby she was carrying was the heir to the Medici fortune.

'You owe it to Sophia to at least try, Katya.'

Katya gasped. The unfairness of her mother's words raged inside her but the overwhelming impotence she had felt from childhood neutralised her rage, her hate. It didn't seem to matter how far away she got from Moscow, her mother's ability to reach across the world and tap into her childhood psyche was astounding.

'Goodbye, Mama,' Katya said, swallowing hard as a rush of bile rose in her throat.

Katya replaced the phone, cutting off her mother's reply. She felt dead inside. Damn her mother. Damn her to hell.

She raised her troubled blue gaze and found Ben watching her.

'Everything OK, *cara*?' he asked softly.

Katya could see the concern in the depths of his eyes. She knew he had gleaned enough from the one-sided Russian conversation to know that it hadn't been a happy family reunion. His kindness was unbearable when she felt so raw inside.

She shook her head. 'Mothers.' She gave him a half-smile. He chuckled and Katya knew he was waiting for her to elaborate. To say more. But…she couldn't. If she'd needed to escape the theatre before the phone call, it was an absolute necessity now.

'See you after lunch,' she said, not waiting for a response.

Ben kicked at the aged paving stones of the Piazza Duomo. He scanned the outdoor cafés thronged with locals and tourists alike in the glorious sunshine, hoping to see Katya sitting at one of them. Gabriella had told him she was coming here and it was only the lunch-break so she couldn't have got too far.

Katya had covered well but he could tell that the phone call from her mother had upset her. He couldn't explain why he felt the need, but he wanted to check if she was OK. He remembered the look they'd exchanged in Lupi's doorway that morning, like she could see all was not well with him, and he wanted her to know that he was sensitive to her emotional state as well.

He decided to do a circuit. The day was nice, the sun beating down, and it felt good to be outdoors. He dodged some young boys kicking a soccer ball around the massive square, his mind preoccupied with Katya's phone call.

It was obvious that Katya had been arguing with her mother and even more obvious from her tone and her body language that she hadn't been happy about talking to her mother in the first place. But she had. And that was something Ben understood all too well. Doing something against your will for the sake of family. Family responsibility.

The *duomo*'s bell marked the hour with its deep chiming and brought him out of his thoughts. His eyes scanned the crowds and inside the different ceramic and tourist shops that bordered the square. Just as he was about to give up, he saw her inside the cameo shop.

He entered, his eyes taking a moment to adjust to the dim light. Katya was talking to a shop assistant, her back bent over the glass-topped counter, a cameo laid out on black velvet before her. She was wearing a gypsy-style skirt and a form-fitting short-sleeved T-shirt that emphasised the petiteness of her frame and the bony ridge of her spine.

Giovanna, the shop assistant, raised her eyes to his and instantly straightened. There weren't too many locals in Ravello who didn't know Count Medici on sight! He held his finger up to his mouth and smiled at her.

She smiled back and Ben saw the invitation in her eyes and wished he didn't feel complete disinterest. What the hell was the matter with him? Giovanna was a very attractive woman and he hadn't been with anyone since before he'd met Katya.

'It's so beautiful,' Katya sighed, unaware of Ben's presence. 'My grandmother had one very similar to this.'

Katya touched the chalky-white surface of the burnished orange cameo. It depicted a curly haired woman in profile, with bare shoulders and a strange, sad kind of smile. She remembered stroking her grandmother's as a child. There weren't that many memories that she recalled fondly but her grandmother starred in every one. Looking at the beautiful oval cameo and recalling the wonderful times it evoked was like a soothing balm after the vileness of her mother's phone call.

She remembered being held to the old woman's ample bosom, the cameo sitting snugly in her grandmother's cleavage, and she remembered feeling safe there. Feeling loved. She'd been seven when her grandmother had passed away and she still recalled how devastated she'd been.

Almost as devastated as the day Olgah had taken the cameo and pawned it. Katya had begged her mother not to, had clung to Olgah's leg as she'd tried to get out the door. But it hadn't stopped her. Katya remembered to this day how bleak and impotent she had felt as her mother had shut the door in her face.

If only she still had the cameo today, she knew what she'd do with it. She would leave it here with Ben, as a parting gift for her child. Something to connect the baby with its mother. And maybe her child could draw comfort from it over the years, as she would have done. Know, hopefully, that Katya loved him or her. Loved her child enough to give it the best life possible.

Ben could see Katya in profile and watched the flicker of emotions play across her face. His breath caught. He'd never seen her look so vulnerable. He could see fondness and happiness and regret mingling in her slight Mona Lisa smile. She looked wistful and sad and very, very young.

He'd never truly realised how shuttered, how in control she

was until he'd seen her like this. She looked vulnerable, un-
certain for the first time since he'd known her. Like he was
seeing the real Katya, the one beneath the bluster and the barbs.

Not even on that magical night that they'd shared had he
seen her like this. What had made her the Katya she was
today? The practical, tough, no-nonsense façade she hid
behind. What had happened to this Katya, the one bent over
the cameo, to make her seem so hard? Had that phone call had
something to do with it?

Ben was intrigued as never before. Whatever the reasons,
seeing her like this made him want to see more. This soft,
female Katya was appealing on levels he'd never known
existed. It made him want to make her happy. Put a smile on
her face. Not a small sad little smile, but a big beaming one.
He wanted to see her glow. And the way she was looking at
that cameo, he knew just how to achieve it.

'We'll take it, thanks, Giovanna,' Ben said, striding over
to the counter and winking at the shop assistant.

He saw Katya's back stiffen and she turned around slowly.
She gave him a look that left him in doubt he was not welcome
in the shop—very different to the warm, flirty welcome
Giovanna had given him. Why the hell did that do more for
him than Giovanna's blatantly sexual smile?

'No, we won't,' Katya said, placing a stilling hand on
Giovanna's, not taking her gaze off Ben.

'You like it.' Ben shrugged. 'Consider it a gift.'

How many men had given her mother gifts? Seduced her
into neglecting her children? Her mother's words rang in her
ears—*if you played your cards right...we'd never have to
worry about money again.* She felt bile rise in her again. She
would not stoop to her mother's level. She'd never taken
anything from a man and she wasn't about to start.

'I don't take *gifts* from men,' she said emphatically.

He blinked. She was angry with him—that was obvious. Her eyes glittered and her mouth was flattened into a thin line. Not the usual reaction he got when offering to buy women jewellery. He sensed he needed to tread carefully. 'It obviously means a lot to you,' he said softly.

'It's eight hundred euros,' Katya said, her voice blunt, her tone unmoved.

'Money is not an issue, *cara*,' he said, smiling gently, still hopeful of breaking through to her, the girl he'd caught a glimpse of. 'Can you wrap it for me?' he asked Giovanna.

'No. Do not wrap it,' Katya said, giving a severe look at the shop assistant. She would rather take cyanide than accept this from Ben. She felt raw on the inside from her mother's barbs and his persistence was rubbing salt into the wounds. 'And do not call me darling,' she snapped, and stormed out of the shop.

'Katya.'

She heard him calling her name but she was too angry to stop. Visions of the trinkets her mother's suitors had bought her flashed before her eyes. She remembered how exhausted she'd been each night, looking after four little ones while her mother had been out. She remembered Sophia getting burned, her sister's dreadful inconsolable screams. They reverberated around her head as she hurried away, they followed her now as they had haunted her for so many years.

She could hear her breath coming in short sharp gasps as she remembered the horror of that day and the crippling panic that had gripped her as her eleven-year-old brain had struggled with the enormity of what had happened. Images she'd thought she'd conquered a long time ago bombarded her as she walked blindly through the piazza, Ben's voice following her.

'Katya.' He caught up, grabbing her arm and halting her.

'Let go of me,' she yelled, blinking back tears she hadn't even known had formed.

Ben held onto her shoulders as she struggled against him. Something was really wrong, she was really upset. He'd never seen her tearful. 'Hey, hey, what's wrong? I'm sorry, OK? You seemed so taken with it. Don't worry about it, it's no big deal.'

She moved close to him, her heart hammering, her chest heaving. 'It is to me,' she said, her voice steely.

She saw the confusion and concern on his face. She could tell he was puzzled by her reaction. Hell, she was puzzled by it. One phone call from her mother and she was eleven years old again! But this was important.

Ben was relieved that she'd stopped trying to resist but he could still feel the tension in her shoulders. His fingers gently massaged the flesh coaxing her to relax. 'I'm sorry,' he said softly.

'I can buy my own jewellry.'

He nodded at her. 'I'm sorry,' he said again. He watched her watch him, her gaze assessing, as if she was searching for the truth in his statement. And then he felt her finally let go and her shoulders sagged against his hands.

'I'm sorry,' she whispered.

Ben gave her a tender smile. Piazza life careened all around them. The sun beat down, locals strolled, tourists snapped photos and shopkeepers touted for trade, but they were oblivious, locked in their own little bubble.

He pulled her gently towards him, half expecting her to resist, but she went without argument and he tucked her against him. She felt good against him, too good, and he wished for a moment that he hadn't done it. But instinct told him it was the right thing to do.

Katya Petrova was a complicated woman. A deceptive

woman. There were layers beneath her prickly surface that obviously ran deep. Holding her close, his heart thudding loudly in his ears, he realised he wanted to explore them. To understand what made her tick, what had made her the woman she was today. What had happened to cause such a meltdown just now? Would she let him in and why did he suddenly care so much?

Katya breathed deeply, inhaling his scent. He smelt like man, like Ben, and she remembered vividly how good it was to be held intimately by him. It was crazy, she couldn't buy into it, but for this moment, as her heartbeat settled down again, it was heavenly.

Soon she would have to pull away and repair the damage she'd done with her little performance. God knew what he thought. And she was going to have to tell him about the baby. Not right now, but soon.

She didn't want to leave it for weeks and weeks now she'd made up her mind. He had a right to know and as soon as she told him, there wouldn't be anything to hide from him any more. She didn't believe in deception, had seen way too much of it growing up, and he couldn't accuse her of a hidden agenda once the truth was out.

'We'd better get back,' Katya said, breaking the embrace.

They both turned towards the clinic and began to make their way back slowly.

'You want to come with me to my villa this weekend?' Ben asked. 'We can go out on *The Mermaid*.'

She looked at him. He had just handed her a golden opportunity. She nodded. 'Yes, thanks. Sounds like fun.'

So…tomorrow. It was set. She'd tell him about the baby tomorrow. And tonight she'd try and find the right words to deliver the shocking news.

pletely shattered. Totally undone. Every female cell in her body had responded to his utter desolation.

He shrugged. 'It was a shock.'

'Well, of course, estranged or not, he was still your brother.'

'No.' Ben shook his head emphatically. 'He stopped being my brother a decade ago.'

Ben turned bleak eyes on her and she shivered despite the warm weather. 'I'm sorry. That's very sad,' she said.

Ben's lips twisted. 'That's life. Come on.' He stood. 'Let's eat and get on our way.'

Ben strode ahead of her and she followed him slowly. Was this why Lucia was so worried about her son? Something had obviously happened between Ben and his brother. Something that had been strong enough to drive a wedge between them for ten years. Something that had persisted, even through death.

Katya caught up with Ben a minute later. He had been stopped by Damul, the father of the two children they had operated on yesterday. The man had tears in his eyes and the biggest, broadest grin Katya had ever seen. He was shaking Ben's hand and gabbling away at him in his own dialect.

Ben spoke back to him in Italian as their hands remained clasped. Katya smiled at Damul, who bestowed another grin on her. She could see the joy behind his tears, how grateful he was, and her smile grew wider. Damul had been through so much. The loss of his wife and the injury to his children, Katya could only imagine how impotent he must have felt.

Damul patted Ben on the back and slowly withdrew, smiling all the way.

'A happy customer,' Katya said, still smiling from Damul's joy.

Ben smiled back. 'It's a good feeling.'

'Yes,' she said, 'it is, isn't it?' To be a part of Ben's g

CHAPTER FOUR

KATYA was awake early, having spent a night rehearsing the words she was going to use. She had a speech prepared and she hoped it was impassioned enough for him to understand that her motives were pure. That she was doing what she was doing for the sake of their baby.

She had no idea how he was going to react, none at all, and thinking about it, trying to second-guess it, was driving her crazy. Katya decided to get up and dressed and go and sit in the garden for a while. She doubted whether her thoughts would be any clearer, but at least she could stare at the Med rather than four walls.

The weather was beautiful outside and Katya could see it was going to be another gorgeous September day. She had a brown sundress on with shoestring straps, and she revelled in the early kiss of the sun on her practically bare shoulders. She could so get used to living here.

She bit into the plump flesh of a peach as she wandered around, trying to settle the nausea that had plagued her the minute she'd stood up. She hoped it wasn't going to be a bad morning-sickness day. If she was going to go on Ben's boat, the last thing she needed was a queasy stoma

The gardens really were magnificent. She had spent most of her lunch hours outside, eating with the other nurses who chose a different terraced level each day to spread out on and soak up some sun. A lot of their patients also ventured out into the gardens and Katya liked the continuity of it all. So different from MedSurg.

She could hear the trickle of water and wondered if the fountains ran continuously or whether they were on timers. It felt good to be thinking inane things. Her mind had been preoccupied all night with such serious matters. Coming outside, getting up, had been a good idea.

Even high in the hills she could see the sun sparkling off the sapphire-blue Med and she drew a deep breath of clean air into her lungs. The beauty was distracting and she sat on a wrought-iron garden chair and soaked it in. She shut her eyes and tipped her face towards the early morning sun.

'Penny for them.'

Katya opened her eyes to find Ben looking down at her. Her heart skipped a beat. He looked so fresh and rested. His hair was damp and curling over his collar at the nape of his neck. The words she'd rehearsed all night spun around in her head. 'Good morning,' she said, in what she hoped sounded like a normal voice.

'*Buongiorno*, Katya. May I join you?'

Katya shuffled over, making room for him on the seat.

'You like our gardens?' he asked.

She nodded. 'They are very beautiful. Did you have someone design them for you or were they already like this?'

'The gardens have been here as long as the villa, for centuries, but they were very unkempt when we bought the property. Mario…' Ben's words trailed off, the familiar ache starting up at the mention of his brother.

Katya waited for him to continue. She'd been there the night Ben had received the news of Mario's death. She had witnessed his devastation firsthand.

'The gardens were Mario's baby. He had this grand vision for them and hired Europe's foremost expert on terraced gardens to help him design what you see today.'

'It must be kind of nice to have a lasting legacy like this, to remind you of your brother,' she said gently.

Ben just stopped himself from snorting. He rarely came into the gardens. Mario was everywhere and some things were just too painful. The last thing he needed to remember was how his brother had betrayed him. How he had discovered Mario and Bianca sharing a passionate kiss not far from here in these very grounds. Somehow the gardens had never seemed quite the same.

'He…did a great job,' Ben acknowledged through tight lips.

Katya looked at him sharply. She detected a slight bitterness to his tone. Maybe he didn't want to talk about his brother? Maybe it was too soon, too raw? Maybe that was what the contessa had alluded to on her first night?

Katya felt guilty that with everything she was going through she had totally forgotten that Ben's brother was dead. 'I'm sorry, Ben, I haven't asked. It's only been a few months—how are you coping with Mario's death?'

This time Ben did snort. 'Don't worry about me, Katya. There was no love lost between Mario and I. We were…estranged when he died.'

So? Did that make a difference when your own flesh and blood died tragically? Would she cry when her mother died? Of course. If for nothing else, over the wasted years, the wasted opportunities. If anything, being estranged made it worse.

'You seemed pretty upset that night.' He had looked com-

dream had been extremely rewarding, even in the little time she'd been there.

He frowned at her. 'Really? I'd have thought it'd be a little too slow for you. I thought you liked the pace and the anonymity of the patch them up and send them on environment?'

So had she. And she did. The high turnover and hectic pace was exhilarating. She thrived on it. And the virtual anonymity of their patients was vital to keep burnout at bay. Being a body part rather than a whole person made the horror of it all easier to process. From a very young age Katya had learned to block her emotions so it was inevitable, almost, that she should gravitate to a work environment where there was no time for emotions.

But suddenly it didn't seem to be the be-all and end-all. Getting to know Lupi and Damul's children and the other kids had been surprisingly gratifying. Maybe it was just her hormones but for the first time in a long time she actually felt like a nurse.

She knew what she did at MedSurg mattered, that without people like her and Gill and Ben, many, many people might have died. But here at the clinic she was learning that making a difference to just one person, one child, could be intensely, intimately rewarding as well.

'Maybe I'm mellowing.' She shrugged.

Ben hooted with laughter, remembering their altercation yesterday. 'I can't quite imagine you mellow.'

She straightened. He was right. She was about to turn his life upside down. She couldn't afford to mellow until her job here was done. She shot him a withering look. 'Don't you forget, Count,' she said, and strode away.

He chuckled and followed her to the staff dining room where they had a quick breakfast. Half an hour later they were on the road to Amalfi and Katya was, once again, clutching the seat as Ben steered the Alfa expertly on the kamikaze roads. She was too frightened to even worry about what the rest of the day would hold, and in a crazy way it was a blessed relief.

When they arrived in Amalfi, Ben parked his car in the harbour car park. The sun reflected off the shiny surfaces of all the sleek white boats and Katya donned her sunglasses. She followed him past rows and rows of aquatic craft before pulling up in front of *The Mermaid*.

'Isn't she beautiful?' he asked.

Katya was pleased to see that Ben had shed his mood from the garden and she gave *The Mermaid* the once-over. She supposed it was beautiful but she was paying more attention to the way the boat bobbed in the water.

'Come on,' he said, grabbing her hand and helping her on-board. 'I'll show you around.'

Ben adored this boat. He'd had every intention of selling her when he'd sold the Ferarri—after all, he hadn't been out in her in a decade—but he just couldn't bring himself to do it. Maybe because it didn't have the same symbolism as the red car had had. Mario hadn't been interested in boats so *The Mermaid* was something that didn't represent his continuous rivalry with his brother. The boat had been truly just about his own pleasure.

As he sat at the helm and refamiliarised himself with the dials, ran his hands over the wheel, he lamented not having found the time to go out in her often. He'd been out in her once since his return to Italy and had been too busy with the Lucia Trust to go again. Maybe if Katya enjoyed herself this weekend, she'd come out with him again?

'Is there a bathroom on this thing?' she asked, her stomach already protesting the slight swell she could feel through the soles of her feet.

'Sure.' He grinned. 'Come on, I'll show you below.'

Katya didn't feel like she was going to vomit—yet. But she wanted to make sure she knew where to head if she did. This boat was shinier than anything she'd ever seen before, and she didn't want to foul it.

She climbed down the stairs, following his lead, and walked into pure luxury. Her feet sank into deep-pile carpet and her eyes took a moment to adjust to the muted light. They were in a lounge area with leather chairs and a coffee-table. A plasma screen dominated the wall the chairs faced.

Ben showed her the galley, which sparkled and shone like everything else. Then he showed her the cabins—two large luxurious ones equipped with huge beds. Beds you could roll over and over and over in. She had a vision of the two of them doing just that, the sheets tangling around their legs. She blinked hard to dispel it as he showed her the decadent *en suites* complete with spas.

'What do you think?' he asked.

Katya reeled. She'd never been amongst such luxury. The splendour of the Lucia Clinic faded in comparison. She felt gauche, like Cinderella at the ball. Her head spun and for a brief moment she thought she was going to lose the contents of her stomach immediately. 'It's like a…palace,' she said.

Ben chuckled. She looked all wide-eyed and he could tell she felt overwhelmed. 'Every woman deserves a palace once in a while, don't you think?' he asked.

Katya wasn't sure about that. It wasn't something she'd ever wished for. She'd wished they'd had more. That her mother had been home more often. That she could have gone to school more often. That they'd had food in their cupboards and a warm house all the time. She'd never even dared to wish for something like this.

And her child was going to be part of all this. Would grow up amongst all these amazing things. Would never know what it was like to feel hungry or cold. Or unloved. This wasn't a life she would ever feel comfortable living, but as much as it dazzled, even scared her, she was pleased that the baby would never have the sort of life she'd endured.

'I guess,' she said quietly. Doubtfully.

'I know you don't feel comfortable with all this,' Ben said, gesturing around him, 'but I swear, if you just let yourself, you'll have a great day.'

Katya looked into his earnest face. He wanted her to like his boat. He wanted her to enjoy herself. She could see it in his keen gaze. She smiled at him then and made a conscious effort to relax. Considering the bombshell she was going to drop at some stage, the least she could do was let him know how much she appreciated him trying to show her a good time.

'OK.' She smiled. 'Aye, aye, Captain.' And she saluted him.

Ben threw back his head and laughed. Somehow he couldn't imagine Katya ever being obedient. It was almost as absurd as her being mellow. 'Let's go back on deck and get under way.'

'Aye, aye, Captain,' she repeated, and joined in as he laughed again.

Katya's enjoyment soon faded as they moved out of the harbour. The Med was flat. It sparkled before them like a carpet of sapphires. Smooth as glass, beautiful blue glass. But the movement of the boat and her hormones were not getting along and they'd only been out for two minutes before Katya knew for sure—this was going to be a bad morning-sickness day.

'How long to your villa?' she asked, gripping the side of the boat, the faint whiff of engine fumes and the wake of another boat kicking her nausea up another notch.

'It's only half an hour from here,' Ben said, concentrating on navigating out of the busy area near Almalfi. 'But I thought I'd take you on a grand tour of the Amalfi coast. You've just got to see Positano from the ocean, it's an amazing aspect. Maybe we can even head to Capri, stay on the boat overnight, head back to the villa in the morning.'

Katya felt her stomach lurch. He looked at her for confirmation of his plans. He looked so excited, like a kid with an ice cream, and she didn't have the heart to ask him to turn the boat around. She nodded and smiled back. Maybe the nausea wouldn't last. Maybe it would be a day when the sickness only actually lasted the morning.

Pity she was feeling so wretched because the view inside the boat was just as spectacular as the view over the water. Ben was wearing some hip-hugging denim shorts. They had frayed hems, and showed off his magnificent long legs. A chocolate polo shirt completed the outfit, the sleeves fitting snugly around his biceps.

His hair blew in the breeze, becoming tousled, and a part of her wanted to walk up behind him, put her arms around his waist and snuggle her body into his. But she knew that any movement at the moment would be catastrophic both to her equilibrium and to her grand plan.

A speedboat passed them, rocking their craft in its wake, and Katya knew she was going to be violently ill. Ben shouted something in Italian but she didn't wait for a translation. She made a mad, rather inelegant dash for the stairs and just made it to the closest bathroom as the contents of her stomach rushed out.

Katya heaved and heaved into the bowl, wishing she was anywhere but here. Moisture welled in her eyes as she continued to retch. She felt cheap and nasty besmirching the beautiful luxury of the most elegant toilet she'd ever been in, but her stomach wouldn't let up and all she could do was cling helplessly to the porcelain and hope it would be over soon.

After what seemed an age she slumped back against the wall and shut her eyes. She could feel herself trembling all over and taste the bitterness of bile in her mouth. She waited until she felt strong enough to stand and clung to the wall as she pushed herself into a standing position.

She was grateful to find a boxed toothbrush and toothpaste in one of the marble vanity drawers and she brushed her teeth until her mouth felt minty fresh again. She looked at her face in the mirror. She looked like hell. Her pale complexion looked even whiter than normal and her blue eyes looked dull. But she felt better as each second passed and her spirits revived with the thought that now she'd vomited, the worst was over.

She could feel the powerful throb of the engine reverberate through her feet as she made her way back through the lounge and up the stairs.

'You weren't joking about the seasick thing, were you?' Ben said as Katya emerged from down below. 'Are you OK?'

'Sure. I feel much better,' she said, placing her foot on the deck. The breeze hit her face and a faint trace of engine fumes assaulted her nostrils. Nausea slammed into her gut and rolled through her intestines. She held up her hand to her mouth. 'I'll be right back.'

Katya made another mad dash to the toilet, again making it just in time. There was nothing left to bring up but it didn't stop her delicate constitution from trying. She felt like her hormones were ringing every last morsel of food from her entire digestive tract.

She vaguely heard the rumble of the engine cut out as she again slumped against the wall. The cessation of movement rallied her equilibrium but she felt as weak as a kitten. All she wanted to do was curl up on one of those heavenly looking plump leather couches she had now seen three times, shut her eyes and sleep through the trip.

'Katya?'

She opened an eye to see Ben standing in the doorway. If she'd have been remotely well, she would have worried about how bad she must look right now, but frankly she couldn't care less if she looked like she'd been dragged through a hedge backwards. 'I'm fine,' she said.

Ben looked down at the distinctly un-fine-looking Katya propped against the toilet wall. She looked like hell. Her blonde feathery fringe was plastered to her forehead, slick with sweat. Her normally pale complexion looked as white as the wall she was leaning against. So much for a great day on the water.

He turned to the vanity in the bathroom, removed a face-cloth from one of the drawers, wet it under the gold-plated tap and wrung it out. He crouched down beside her and pressed the cloth to her forehead. Her eyes flicked open briefly.

'I'm fine,' she mumbled.

'You look like hell,' he said. Ben mopped her sweaty brow with the cool cloth and trailed it over the rest of her face, across her parched lips and down her neck.

Katya murmured something in Russian and he felt as if she'd run her fingers over his stomach muscles. He'd never seen her helpless like this, so...docile. He'd never seen any sign of weakness from her, apart from yesterday afternoon in the cameo shop. It seemed he was seeing a different side to Katya the more time he spent with her.

The urge to sweep her up in his arms and protect her from her demons was overwhelming. Had she eaten something at breakfast that had been off? Was she actually really ill? Or was she really just not a seafarer? He needed to examine her in case she was developing a serious medical condition.

He tossed the facecloth over his shoulder and swept her up in one easy move into his arms. She barely protested. She felt floppy, like deadweight, even though he managed her slight proportions easily. He eased her gently down onto the leather couch and then went back to the bathroom to remoisten the facecloth.

Ben returned quickly and mopped her face again, folding the cloth and placing it along her forehead. She felt warm and he was worried now that this was something serious.

'Katya. Katya?' he said, speaking quietly, stroking his fingers gently down her arm.

Her eyes flicked open briefly. 'Mmm. That's nice,' she sighed.

Ben chuckled. She was right about that. 'I'm going to give you a quick once-over, Katya,' he said, 'just to check everything's OK.'

Katya was floating along in a nice hazy world. She could hear his voice and it was as sexy as ever and she wanted to wrap it around her like a feather duvet and go to sleep. She felt his long, lean surgeon's fingers at her wrist and felt sure he must be able to feel the flutter of her heart at his touch.

She felt his hands on her abdomen. They were deft, methodical, poking and prodding. 'Mind the baby,' she said, slipping into her native tongue as her hazy mind transmitted his non-sexual touch into a lover's caress.

Katya's eyes flew open. Had she said that in English or Russian? 'What are you doing?' she demanded, half sitting, displacing his hands, which were moving slowly and systematically lower. The baby! The baby! She was instantly awake.

'It's OK,' Ben said soothingly. 'I was just seeing if you had any abdominal tenderness.'

'I told you, I'm fine,' she said, removing his hands.

'You don't look so fine,' Ben said impatiently. 'You were out of it there for a minute. Did you eat something off this morning?' he asked, placing his hands against her stomach again.

'Nothing,' she protested, batting his hands away. 'We ate the same things. I'm not good on boats, that's all,' she protested weakly.

'Please, don't insult me. You couldn't get water any flatter unless you were in the bathtub.'

Katya watched as Ben started to pace and rattled off a number of things it could be.

'I don't think it's appendicitis. There's no rebound tenderness,' he muttered. 'No…you had the ham on your roll and I didn't,' he said, turning to her. 'Maybe it was off and you've contracted food poisoning.' Ben raked his fingers through his hair. 'Oh, God! How many staff and patients have had that ham today? This sort of thing doesn't happen at the Lucia Clinic. I'll have to ring the chef,' he said, striding over to the old-fashioned marble-handled telephone and dialing the clinic number.

Katya watched him in dismay. 'Ben, it's nothing.'

He held his hand over the receiver. 'Of course it is,' he said impatiently. 'People can't come to our clinic and get food poisoning. As soon as I'm done here, we'll head back to Amalfi and we'll go to the hospital. You may need rehydration.'

Katya couldn't believe how this was escalating out of control. She could see it becoming an international incident before her eyes. 'Ben, for God's sake, put the phone down. I'm pregnant, that's all.'

She hadn't meant to blurt it out like that. She had her speech all prepared. Had lain awake all last night, perfecting it. And in a matter of seconds she'd blown it out of the water. She watched his face as her words sank in.

'What did you say?' he asked, as he slowly replaced the receiver.

Katya sighed. She felt too wretched now to give him the whole spiel. She swung her legs around and sat up gingerly. At least with the boat now stopped, her stomach seemed to be more settled. 'I'm having your baby,' she said, her voice stronger now.

Ben stared at her, not even really seeing her as her words slowly filtered through. Baby? Was she insane? 'But…how?'

Katya could see she'd really thrown him. She'd never seen him look pale—ever. But he did now. And he was clutching the phone like he was going to fall over if he let go. She understood his question was rhetorical so she didn't bother answering it. She just sat and watched him, waiting for it to sink in further.

'Are you sure?' he asked.

Katya nodded patiently. It was a fair enough question. She'd spent a good week in total disbelief. 'I've taken three tests and been throwing up every day for two months.'

Ben blinked. This couldn't be happening. Him? A father? He didn't know how to be a father. He just couldn't get his head around it. 'Are you sure it's mine?' Thinking about it, they hadn't used any protection. It had been such a spontaneous act and he'd been so shaken that it hadn't even occurred to him. He'd just needed to be close to her, to hold her, to blot out the awful events and years of stupid, futile anger.

Katya felt the question slam into her even though it was delivered with no malice or accusation. The hairs on the back of her neck prickled. No way! He didn't get to question the paternity. 'I'm one hundred per cent sure,' she said rising, her hands curling into fists by her side. 'I was a virgin that night, Ben.'

Ben took the second body blow just as hard. His thoughts reeled. 'You were?' Shouldn't he have been able to tell? Had he been that caught up in his own grief and regret that he hadn't been paying attention to her cues?

'*Da*,' she said shortly.

'But…but I didn't… I couldn't… You seemed…'

'Oh, for God's sake, Ben,' she snapped.

That was it, Ben had to sit down. He walked over to the lounge opposite Katya's and sank into the plush leather. 'How do you get to twenty-seven and still be a virgin?' he asked.

Katya snorted. Growing up in her house, it had been easy. She'd lived with a woman who used sex as a commodity. Sure, deep down Katya really believed that Olgah had truly just wanted to be loved, but Katya had seen too many men come and go and leave her mother broken-hearted to trust any man. As a mere child she had picked up the pieces once too often. Held her mother, stroked her prematurely grey hair, while she had sobbed her heart out.

As a child, Katya had been frightened and bewildered by her mother's ups and downs. As an adult, her mother's example had taught Katya that weaknesses destroyed you. Consequently, she'd never let her guard down enough to have a relationship. Being intimate? Forget it!

Ben had been a complete one-off for her. A totally out-of-character thing for her to do but he'd been so shaken, so devastated that she hadn't even questioned her actions. She had just known on some intuitive female level that Ben needed comfort and had known how to provide it. The questions and the reprimands had come soon enough. The next morning, she had felt no better than her mother.

'Upbringing,' Katya said dismissively as she sat, wanting to rehash that night as little as possible. 'Anyway, that's not the point. The point is I'm pregnant. I'm sorry, I didn't plan to tell you this way.'

Ben shook his head to clear it. She was right. The point was, he was going to be a father. The thought was no less horrifying than it had been minutes ago. But something was clearer. 'That's why you're here,' he said. 'You came to tell me you were pregnant?'

'*Da.*' Katya nodded.

Ben could feel his thoughts coming back on line now. Things were starting to make sense. And yet they weren't. 'Why? You could have just rung me.'

'Because I don't want the baby.'

Ben took a moment to absorb her answer. It seemed they were back to not making any sense. 'So why didn't you just have a termination?' When he thought about it, it was exactly the thing that practical, sensible, no-nonsense Katya would do. Why not, if she didn't want the baby? Want his baby. *She didn't want his baby?*

Katya shook her head. 'Tried. Couldn't.'

Ben's brow puckered. He felt like he was running in quicksand and sinking. 'What do you mean, couldn't? You couldn't get in to a clinic?'

'I mean I made the appointment, I sat in the waiting room, they called my name and I just couldn't go through with it.' Katya rubbed her stomach. She remembered the moment—the precise moment. The nurse calling her name again and again and knowing, just knowing that she couldn't do it. For better or for worse she had given this baby life, and she couldn't take it away.

Ben heard the husky note to her voice and noted her hand movements. The quicksand solidified a little. How many pregnant women had he seen repeat the same action? Katya's stomach was still flat, no baby bump at all, yet she had the action down pat. She sounded surprised by the turn of events and he could imagine how her inability to see something she'd organised all the way through would have turned her neat, practical world upside down.

But nothing changed the fact that growing inside her was his baby. His flesh and blood. He felt a strange sense of possession and found himself thankful that Katya hadn't been able to go through with the termination.

'So where do we go from here?' he asked.

Katya took a deep breath, forgoing her speech for the direct route. 'I want you to raise the baby.'

Curiouser and curiouser. 'Me?' he said, trying to wrap his head around everything that had come out of her mouth in the last couple of minutes.

'Well, you are the father,' Katya said bluntly.

The father. He was going to be a father. He felt the enormity of that simple statement hit him. How could they have been so careless? He couldn't be a father. He hadn't even been a good brother. Surely a much lesser role? He'd ignored all Mario's overtures, closed himself off to a relationship he'd invested in since birth. He'd closed himself off to any kind of love for so long now. Did he even have the capacity for it any more?

'And how do you envision that will work?' he asked, as his brain madly tried to keep up with the ever-changing plot.

Now, this was a topic she could talk on. This was what she'd been planning for over a month. 'I have a plan.'

She did? 'OK then.' He rubbed his hands through his hair. 'Let's hear it.'

'I'll stay here until the baby is born. After the birth, you can take over the baby's care.'

Ben could see her face become animated. She'd obviously put a lot of thought into this. 'And you?'

Katya shrugged. 'Back to MedSurg, of course.'

Just like that? She could seriously just walk away from her own child? His reticence he could understand. But, Katya? She was the mother. Wasn't that innate? How could she reject their child? 'Why don't you want the baby?'

Katya shook her head emphatically 'Why doesn't matter.'

Ben had the feeling, watching her caress her stomach, that 'why' mattered very much. 'It does to me.'

Katya wrestled with how much to tell him. He didn't need to know all the gory details, just the basics. She sighed. 'From the age of eight until I left home at twenty, I raised three sisters and a brother. I'm mothered out.'

Ben absorbed her stunning statement silently. He caught a brief glimpse of the eight-year-old Katya before her shutters came down. 'Your mother?' he asked.

'Left it up to me,' Katya said, and stared at the floor, not daring to elaborate. How could someone who had grown up with everything—emotionally and financially—ever understand the gritty reality of her childhood?

Five little words spoke volumes to Ben. They were brief and clipped and he noted she couldn't even meet his gaze. Suddenly the whole Katya persona was making so much more sense. Her practicality, her harshness, her bluntness. She would have needed to be all those things to mother four children as a mere child herself.

And her conversation with her mother on the phone yesterday was another piece in the crazy Katya puzzle that was becoming clearer. But looking at her as she cradled their baby with her protective pose, like a lioness protecting her young, he knew he was just scratching the surface. Obviously her childhood had left scars.

'At least you know how,' he said in a soft voice.

Katya saw a flash of Sophia's terror and pain and clamped

down on the memory before it developed sound. 'Trust me, Ben. I wouldn't be any good for this baby.'

'What makes you think I would be any better?' Sure, he could provide for it. But giving himself up completely to another human being, as babies demanded, was a terrifying thought. He'd done that once already and he too had been left with scars.

'Because you have Lucia. You had a fantastic role model and an idyllic childhood—none of which I had. And I see that reflected in the way you've been with Lupi—it's innate in you. I've watched you with Lupi, Ben. You're good with her. And she adores you and so will this baby. And you can give it things I can't.'

'I can't give it a mother's love,' he said.

Katya gripped her abdomen more firmly his words penetrating like bullets, shredding her fortitude. As long as it had love, did it matter whether the source was from the mother or the father? 'I meant material stuff.'

'Like Ferraris and Learjets?'

Katya shook her head, feeling her ire rise. He made her feel like a gold-digger. 'You think I give a damn about expensive status symbols? You think I got pregnant to bleed you dry?'

'I'm sorry,' he said, holding up his hands. 'That was uncalled for.' Ben massaged his forehead. He hadn't meant his words to sound so judgmental. He just couldn't believe his life was suddenly spinning out of control. He'd left Italy a decade ago to get back control over his life and feeling that all slip away again was frustrating.

And he'd be damned if he'd let it take over a second time. He needed to take it back again. And not by running but by staying and taking the only option open to him. The one thing that his traditionalist background demanded. Katya was having his baby. Wanted him to raise it. Then it had to be on his terms. He wasn't going to let another woman turn his life upside down.

He looked at her, her blue eyes still glowering at him, her hand still firmly in place on her stomach. She said she didn't want their baby but her body language said differently. And despite his shock, he couldn't suppress a tiny faint glow deep inside that already connected him to his child. Maybe they'd both been given a chance to overcome their pasts?

'I think we should get married.'

CHAPTER FIVE

KATYA blinked. Her hand stilled on her stomach. 'What did you say?'

Ben couldn't blame her for her shocked expression. He was kind of shocked himself. The whole morning had been one mind-bending revelation after the other. He certainly hadn't come away this morning expecting to ask Katya to marry him. But his old-fashioned values, beliefs ingrained into him by his mother and his upbringing, overrode everything.

They were having a baby—it deserved to be legitimate. Even though his faith in marriage and family had been destroyed a decade ago. Even though Katya wanted nothing to do with the baby. The baby hadn't asked to exist and it deserved no less than any other child. It deserved the right beginning.

'I said, we should get married.'

Katya was lost for words. *Had he gone completely mad?* He was looking at her calmly—no signs of obvious insanity. He wasn't frothing at the mouth or going cross-eyed. What the hell did marrying him have to do with the baby? The thought was as horrifying as it was tantalising.

'You?' she spluttered. 'Bendetto Medici, the playboy count? Get married?'

He shrugged. 'You're pregnant. The baby's mine. It may be old-fashioned but it's the right thing to do.'

Katya blinked again. Old-fashioned? *Try archaic!* 'In the Dark Ages, maybe.'

'I'm a traditionalist.' He shrugged again.

Katya felt bitter laughter bubble in her chest and it was out before she could check it. It sounded harsh in the confines of the cabin. 'This from the man who famously spent one of his leave periods from MedSurg dating every swimwear model he could locate?'

Ben could have been deaf and blind and still wouldn't have missed her mocking tone. Her harsh judgment of him rankled. He was far removed from the man he used to be. 'Dismissing me again, Katya?'

She stood up and pushed herself away from the lounge, putting some distance between herself and the dark, danger-ous glitter of his eyes. She paced over to the window and looked out. This was crazy. Crazy! The Med shimmered and stretched out before her and she turned back lest her now settled stomach decided to change its mind.

'No.'

She'd decided long ago, after witnessing her mother's emo-tional destruction every time a relationship ended, that she'd be far better off without a man. She'd learned the hard way that true commitment and love were elusive and rare and she'd sworn to never settle for less. Never marry for less. Certainly not someone who felt it was his duty and respon-sibility. *All or nothing*. It had to be all or nothing. And she wouldn't compromise, not even for the baby.

Ben wasn't surprised. But he wasn't deterred either. 'Yes.'

Katya shook her head emphatically. He looked so sexy, pinning her to the deck with his brown-eyed stare. She shivered. She was pregnant and had just thrown up her entire stomach contents but when he looked at her, her toes curled. 'No.'

The more she resisted, the more determined he became. 'So, let me see,' he said quietly, observing her hand-on-tummy stance, 'you expect to have our baby then leave it with me with no legally binding contract? Nothing to say that the baby is mine? Do you want our baby to have my name, Katya?'

Katya let his words sink in. For all her planning, she hadn't got that far. Did she? Did she want their baby to have its father's name or hers? What was the point of Ben raising the baby, of her baby growing up in Italy with its father with all the financial security she could dream of, if the child had her name? Whether she liked it or not, she was having a Medici. Wasn't it this baby's birthright to claim its father's name?

'We don't have to marry to give this baby your name.'

'No, but it makes everything a hell of a lot easier. It legitimises this baby's birth better than any other legal process. Both in the eyes of the people and the law. I don't want there to ever be any questions about this baby's paternity. It has rights to my title and the Medici fortune. Everything has to be above board and a marriage is the simplest, easiest way to achieve this.'

Ben finished, congratulating himself on such clear thinking. He wasn't actually sure of the legalities concerning illegitimate children and the line of succession but considering how rattled he was he was surprised he'd been so comprehensive. So concise. But suddenly every word he spoke was important. Part of him, the one per cent that wasn't horrified, the one per cent traditionalist, was already completely committed to this baby.

Katya Petrova was pregnant with his child. *His child.* The Medici heir. And whether it was the male in him or the Italian in him, that meant something. When he had been young and foolish and in love with Bianca he had imagined himself with many children. Had anticipated it, eagerly. Then life had happened and his dream had been destroyed but now, whether he liked it or not, his dream was becoming a belated reality. And he had to face his responsibilities.

Katya blinked. She knew the words he had spoken were the truth. She wanted her child to be legitimate too. She didn't want there to ever be any doubt or whispers. She thought about the whispers she had grown up with. The neighbours who had disapproved of her mother's lifestyle. Five children with no fathers. The gossip. The judgmental stares.

Marrying Ben would tidy up any nasty loose ends. But a marriage would be harder to walk away from. And she couldn't stay. For the sake of her baby, she had to be far, far away.

He had to know that her being involved with this baby was not going to happen. She raised her head and looked him straight in the eye. 'A marriage would mean a divorce. I can't stay after I've had the baby,' she said.

Ben saw the finality in her blue gaze. For some reason she truly believed that this baby would be better off without her. 'Why, Katya? Would being married to me be that awful?'

Oh, God! Awful? On the contrary. She shut her eyes briefly and thought about waking up to his beautiful face every morning. Having his lazy smile and slumberous gaze the first thing she saw every day. It was a delicious thought. A seductive thought.

'I can't be a mother.'

'Because you're mothered out,' he said. Somehow he didn't think that was it. There had to be more than that. As prickly as she could be, abandoning a child just didn't ring true.

She heard the disbelief in his voice. It sounded like such a paltry excuse when he said it like that. But he hadn't lived her life. If he could have just walked a mile in her shoes, he'd understand. But if you're born with a silver spoon in your mouth, how could you possibly understand a life of poverty?

'*Da*,' she said. *Let him think what he liked.*

'I don't believe you,' he said. 'You may not be the softest person I know but underneath your hard exterior, there is a deeply compassionate woman, Katya. I know that because you showed me that woman the night I heard about Mario. The one night I needed comfort and you gave it to me. Unquestioningly. I know that woman could never walk away from a child. Especially her own child.'

Katya just stopped herself from gaping. One night of passion and Ben had seen the person beneath the surface. The Katya she was deep down, beneath the blunt, unemotional façade. The Katya she'd been before her mother had decided to give her responsibilities beyond her years. 'You wouldn't understand,' she said dismissively

'Try me,' he countered.

Katya sighed. 'It doesn't matter, Ben.'

Ben snorted. 'I'm sorry, Katya, it does. You want me to take on a child that you're not prepared to. Give years of my life that you're not prepared to. Convince me.'

Katya looked at him helplessly. How could a man of Ben's background understand? Her hands shook. Baring her soul, telling him everything was too exposing.

'I'd be bad at it.'

'Rubbish.'

Katya's head shot up at his tone. She shook her head. 'You don't know me,' she said. 'You think one night in your arms and you know me?'

He ignored her. If he kept at it, he was sure she'd tell him the real reason. 'I know you're strong. I know you're tough. I know you're capable enough, stubborn enough, fierce enough to do this by yourself.'

Katya shook her head emphatically. 'I've seen how hard it is for a single mother. What a struggle it is to raise a child and juggle work and home commitments. I know how hard it is financially and emotionally. I don't want to be that kind of mother.'

He noted her look of grim determination. Katya's life had obviously been very hard. But despite that she obviously cared about the quality of her mothering. That didn't strike him as someone who didn't care. He sensed he was getting closer and closer to the real reason. 'What kind of mother do you want to be?'

Katya glared at him. She was not going to fall for that. 'I don't want to be any kind of mother.'

'Why?' he persisted.

Why didn't he just leave it alone? 'Because,' Katya said exasperated, 'I'd be really bad at it.'

'Why?' Ben asked again. 'You said yourself you've already raised four babies, one would have thought you'd be highly experienced at it.'

Yeah, right. Katya was sure Sophia would beg to differ. 'I did what I had to do,' she said. 'Doesn't mean I was any good at it.'

Ben watched Katya pluck at the leather beading on the arm of the lounge. Her gaze was downcast, her movements seemed agitated and he suddenly wondered if something bad had happened. 'Katya,' he said, 'talk to me.'

Katya was lured into looking at him by the raw inflection in his voice. He was looking at her with a soft compassionate gaze and she wanted to crawl into his lap and tell him everything. About all the hard years and the guilt.

The terrible guilt she still felt today over her sister's injuries. Even though Sophia was leading a happy and productive life.

She shook her head. 'It's OK for you, Ben. You had a great role model. Lucia is loving and supportive. You probably even had a father at some stage.'

'Not really,' he said. 'My father died when I was one. I never really knew him.'

'I bet your mother adored him, though, right?'

Ben smiled and nodded, remembering the many happy memories his mother had recounted over the years. 'They were very happy. My mother misses him very much.'

Katya nodded. 'I can tell.' The contessa looked like a woman who had been well loved. 'My mother's not like that. She's…different. Life hasn't been so good to her and really, as role models go, she was lousy. So I don't know how to be a mother. Not a good one, anyway.'

Ben was getting a clearer and clearer picture. Katya was the product of her upbringing. But he couldn't get past her hand still absently stroking her abdomen. She may have talked herself out of it but there was something in her actions, in the way she was launching into this crazy plan, that told him she didn't want to walk away from the baby. And if he agreed to Katya's proposal, if raising their child became his responsibility, then surely he'd be remiss if he didn't demand the best? And surely that was two parents?

'You don't have to do it alone, *cara*. I'll be there to help you.'

Katya stared at him, captivated by the promise in his words. But how often had she heard her mother's men say the same thing? Years of ingrained mistrust couldn't be undone so easily.

If she stayed, if she married him, what would happen to the child when it all fell apart? Like her mother's relationships always had? Would their child be forced to pick up the pieces as she had done? Did she want to inflict that on her baby? Repeat the cycle?

Katya shook her head again before she did something stupid like say yes. 'No.' She must not let a count with long eyelashes and silky promises ruin her focus. 'But I'm pleased it will have a father,' she said, rubbing her tummy again. 'I didn't have a father…I missed that. No doubt you did, too.'

Yes, he had. But he'd had a mother. Probably the only person more important than the father in a child's life. 'Yes, I did. But a child needs a mother more. What about breast-feeding? Don't you want the best start in life for our child?'

Katya swallowed as an image of her with Ben's baby snuggled in close rose before her. She could see its dark downy hair and almost feel the pull of its hungry mouth against her breast. 'Plenty of babies are bottle-fed in this world. If that's the worst that can happen, it'll be doing OK.'

Try as he may, Ben just couldn't get his head around a woman rejecting her baby. 'Don't you want this baby, love this baby with every cell in your body?'

Katya felt his words claw at her soul. She didn't expect him to understand her motivations. She cleared her throat. 'This is not about me not loving the baby, Ben. Why do you think I couldn't terminate the pregnancy? But I love it enough to know that I can't look after it. Trust me, it will be much better off without me.'

'All this baby needs is for you to love it, Katya. Nothing else.'

He made it sound so simple. But she'd loved Sophia. And ultimately that hadn't meant anything. It hadn't stopped her getting hurt. Nearly dying. Being permanently scarred.

'No, Ben, trust me, babies can't live on love alone.'

Ben clenched his hands into fists. He was getting tired of

her vague insinuations. He knew she wasn't deliberately trying to frustrate him, that there was something deep down that she couldn't share, that was too horrible for her to talk about. And he knew how that felt. How guilt and anger and circumstances in life made you someone that you didn't want to be or never thought you would turn into.

'What are your other options?' he asked. 'If I say no, what's your plan B?'

Katya felt her heart pounding in her chest. He wouldn't. Would he? 'Adoption,' she said.

Ben felt as if she had slapped him. His head was filled with a mix of emotions all whizzing around, clashing into each other until he didn't know how he felt any more. But he knew how he felt about this. Would she seriously give his baby away to complete strangers? Not that he had a problem with adoption, but his baby? 'Really?' he asked.

She heard the incredulity in his voice. 'It's not my preferred option, Ben. But you have to understand—I can't do this.'

Ben nodded slowly. Suddenly, he believed her. He got it. He really got it now. She was deadly serious. It was him or some stranger raising his child. He rejected it immediately, the traditionalist emerging again. This was his baby. *His baby.* He couldn't let anyone else raise it.

For some reason she really thought she couldn't do it. Some reason that she couldn't tell him about. It was frustrating but maybe she just needed a bit of time. Maybe the marriage would give her a different perspective?

He nodded slowly. 'OK. I'll do it. But only if you agree to marry me.'

Katya felt her body rock with a maelstrom of emotions. Ben had said yes. She had accomplished her goal. But at what cost? She knew everything he said made sense but if she married him, she'd be walking away not just from her baby but from a marriage, too.

'Why,' she asked, 'why do you want to complicate your life by marrying me?'

'Oh, and you think a child won't complicate it?'

She gave him a frustrated stare. 'Don't you think marrying for a child is wrong?'

He shrugged. 'Plenty of couples do it.'

'And plenty of them fail,' she pointed out. 'Don't you want to marry for higher ideals? Like love?'

He snorted. 'Love? What's that? I don't believe in it. All love does is make you blind to things you should see and makes you see things that aren't there.'

Katya blinked. *And she thought she was cynical?* Could she marry a man who didn't believe in love? Even for a few short months? She may have grown up in the gritty reality of life but somewhere beneath her tough exterior there was still a tiny part of her, a remnant of a romantic eight-year-old, who still dreamt of a Prince Charming on a white charger. Who demanded it.

'And what do we tell people when I leave the marriage after the baby's born? If we marry, we give everyone involved a false promise. Can you lie to everyone about that? Can you lie to your mother?'

Ben hesitated. Could he? Could he look his mother in the eye? 'Married or not, they're going to have an expectation that our relationship is going to last longer than a few months,' he said. 'I'm a Medici, they'll have expectations.'

Katya shrugged her slim shoulders. 'Let them.'

'People around here will expect us to marry.'

'I can't, Ben. I won't. I'll do whatever else you ask. I'll sign anything you want to grant you legal recognition as the father of the baby. You can get a paternity test. I'll stay here till it's born. Hell, I'll live with you, if that helps. But I will not marry you.'

Ben heard the finality in her voice. And he believed her. She looked grim and solemn and resolute. 'You're making a mistake,' he said grimly.

She shook her head emphatically. 'No, Ben, I'm not. This is probably the only thing I'm doing right. You see, I have no control over being pregnant. Over this situation. Not now. And if this hadn't have happened, we'd probably never have seen each other again. But I do have control over this. Over who I marry. My faith in marriage is fairly non-existent, I'm afraid. But I do know that I can't settle for less than one hundred per cent love and commitment. I've seen firsthand how that can destroy someone.'

'I can promise you, you will have one hundred and ten per cent commitment from me, Katya.'

Katya laughed harshly. 'What, until I leave?'

He nodded. 'For as long as you stay.'

And then what? Back to the swimwear models? 'Can you promise me love?'

Ben blinked and felt his heart pounding in his chest. An image of Bianca and Mario locked together in a passionate kiss swam before him. Love? What the hell was love? 'Maybe…over time…'

Great. Just like her mother. Waiting around, wasting her life in futile relationships, hanging on for those three magic words? 'Relax, Ben, it's OK. You don't love me. I don't love you. We're just two people who were irresponsible and are facing the consequences. But that only gives you the right to this baby. It doesn't give you the right to me.'

Katya raised her head and held it up proudly. The tradition-alist in him might be forcing him to be noble but the eight-year-old girl in her, the one who'd had all her dreams crushed into the dirt, was stubbornly shaking her head, refusing to give away her last childhood fantasy.

Ben took a moment to digest her words. She really was serious about leaving the child for him to raise. He could see the determined jut of her chin. This was obviously a deal-breaker for her. He quickly weighed up his options. If he insisted, forced her hand, would she leave taking his baby with her? Go through with her plans to have it adopted?

Or could he pull back and try and convince her in the time between now and the baby's birth that their child needed a mother as well as a father? Gently, slowly, surely work away at her, get to know her and help her to see that she *could* be a mother to the baby? Even if they never married, surely Katya staying was the best scenario possible? He had about six months.

He nodded. 'OK, fine,' he conceded. 'We'll play it your way.'

Katya watched his face, searching it for any insincerity, any hesitancy. All she saw was openness and acceptance. She felt all the tension that had been holding her upright since she'd found out about the baby leave her body. Katya gratefully sagged back into the soft leather of the chair. She had done it. She had secured the best possible outcome for her child. What happened from now on didn't matter.

Now it was done, there was a moment of awkwardness. 'If you want to get a test organised and some papers drawn up, I'll sign them,' she said.

He nodded. 'I'll see to it. I'll make sure you're provided for as well.'

Katya felt her heartbeat slow for a few seconds before it sped up and a spurt of anger surged through her bloodstream. This was the second time he'd try to buy her. 'Like payment, Ben?' she asked, her voice low.

'No,' he protested quickly. 'No. I just meant…I don't want the mother of my child to have to struggle.'

Katya could see his good intentions written all over his handsome face and her anger dissipated. She sighed. 'I don't want anything from you, Ben. I never have. Not money or property or anything else. I'll be just fine. I was fine before you and I'll be fine after you.' *Hopefully.* 'All I need is your assurances that you will love and care for our child.'

Ben believed her. She truly was a woman who didn't seem to need anyone. Sincerity oozed from every pore of her body. Katya Petrova was a proud woman. Even a legitimate chance to improve her status was rejected. 'On my family's honour, Katya,' he assured her, 'I will be the best father I can be.'

'Thank you. That's all I want.'

Silence stretched between the two of them. Katya wasn't sure what they should do next. What did people do after they'd haggled over the future of their baby and their lives? Shake on it?

A few more moments passed. Ben roused himself from his still spinning thoughts. 'How are you feeling now?' he asked. 'Do you think your stomach could stand the trip back? We may as well get the ball rolling. We'll go to Positano and tell Mamma.'

Ben stopped and grinned for the first time since Katya had flipped his world on its head. 'She'll be ecstatic.' *Until she finds out about the whole no-wedding thing, anyway.*

Katya felt a ghost of a smile flit across her lips as she imagined Lucia clapping her hands in glee.

'How about your mother? Have you told your family?'

Katya heard her mother's words again about being nice to Ben and she shuddered, thinking about it. She wasn't going to tell her mother about the baby ever. Olgah was not going to get a chance to ingratiate herself with a rich Italian count.

'No.'

Ben regarded her seriously for a few moments, her expression shuttered.

'Katya, she's our baby's grandmother.'

'No.'

He nodded. 'OK.' Now was not the time for pushing. 'Do you reckon you're up to taking the boat to Positano or do you want to head back in to Amalfi and drive?'

Katya looked at both alternatives disparagingly. Neither was particularly attractive. But her stomach was feeling much more settled now and at least on the sea they had more room than on those narrow twisting roads.

'You really have to see Positano from the sea. I think it's the best aspect. It gives you a true appreciation of its magnificence.'

'OK,' Katya agreed, following him up on deck. Whatever. She couldn't believe that after all that had transpired that Ben could calmly talk about other things. Her head was spinning, barely able to formulate a coherent thought.

But he was right, the sea aspect was amazing. She sat on one of the side seats, the breeze blowing her hair, and watched the world go by as the powerful boat ate up the distance. Her stomach never quavered once and Katya actually enjoyed the warm sun on her face and arms.

He pointed out different areas of interest as they passed by and Katya took in the incredible edifices of the villas lining the cliff faces. They clung to the craggy rocks, some new, some almost as old-looking as the mountains themselves. The sun beat down, bathing the scenery in an impossibly bright light, the villas almost glowing.

Each house seemed to have stairs cut into the stone of the cliffs that zigzagged their way down the rock face until they reached concrete platforms at the bottom. Many of the residents were availing themselves of these private balconies, using them not just for sunbathing but as a springboard into the inviting blue of the Med. Some of the people even waved at Ben as the boat sped by.

'That's mine,' he said, raising his voice to be heard over the engine as he pointed to an impressive white villa dominating the rock face.

Katya stared at it. It was huge, sprawling along the cliff top, its clean white lines and arched windows elegant. Purple bougainvillea crept along the façade on one side, a colourful foil to the stark whiteness. It too had steps that led down the cliff to the sea below, with more bougainvillea creeping along the iron railings, blazing a trail of colour down to the sea.

'That's where we'll live,' he said.

She turned and looked at him. He returned her searching stare with an unflinching brown gaze. So, he was taking her up on her offer to cohabit? She turned back quickly, her heart beating a mad tattoo. What would it be like living in this beautiful white home? It looked like a palace sitting atop the cliffs in all its dazzling white glory and Katya found it difficult to digest. In a couple of short months her whole life had been turned upside down and she wasn't sure about anything.

She had a moment's yearning for her previous life as the villa passed from her direct line of sight. At least she'd known who she was before she'd become pregnant. She'd been her own person. Now she was having a baby and was about to live in a palatial villa in Italy with a one-hundred-and-eighty degree view of the Mediterranean in the company of a devilishly good-looking count. She knew how to be Katya Petrova, poor Russian nurse. She didn't know how to be this Katya. *Ben's Katya.*

The scenery continued to dazzle her as the boat sped on.

Positano appeared in the distance, nestled on the shoreline at the feet of the soaring mountains behind. As it grew bigger she could see the alternating orange and blue lines of the deckchairs adorning the front, a striking contrast to the black stones of the beach.

Rows and rows of villas clung to the two main cliffs in a haphazard, colourful display, each one on top of the next, crammed in so the rock of the cliff wasn't visible. Just buildings. Private homes sharing space with tourist hotels. The impressive *duomo* nestled between, dominating the seafront. People, locals and tourists alike, cluttered the beach, swam in the sea or sunned themselves.

Katya had a moment of complete disconnectedness. She was really here. In a beautiful Italian seaside resort village. An Italian count beside her. It seemed too incredible to be true. Never even as child had she dreamed this big.

Ben cut the engine and dropped anchor a little way from the shore. Katya watched as he shaded his eyes from the sun and searched through the crowd of people. He spotted who he wanted on the short rickety wooden pier, then put his fingers in his mouth and let out a short sharp whistle. 'Hey, Marco!'

A man turned and Ben waved at him. The man dived into the sea and swam quickly to one of the many small boats that bobbed calmly nearby. He hauled himself in, pulled up the anchor and started the motor.

'You ready?' Ben asked, turning to Katya as Marco's small boat with the outboard motor grew closer.

She nodded and stood just as Marco reached *The Mermaid* and pulled up alongside.

'Hey, Marco, my friend. Thanks for the lift,' Ben said in Italian.

'Anything for you, Count,' Marco replied, grinning.

'This is Katya.' Ben introduced them in English and Marco held out his hand to help Katya into his boat.

Marco said something in Italian to Ben and they both laughed. '*Bella*,' he said to Katya and grinned. 'Benedetto is a lucky man.'

Ben roared with laughter and said something else in Italian and they both laughed again as Ben stepped into the boat as well. Katya sat on one of the wooden cross seats and Ben plonked himself beside her and placed his hand on her knee and smiled down at her.

It was such a dazzling smile, Katya forgot to breathe, and she certainly forgot to tell him to take his hand off her. It seemed that Ben wanted to portray them as a young, in-love couple and Katya gave him a small smile back. If he thought it was important to pretend to be something they weren't then she could go along with that. As long as he remembered that their act had a definite end date.

They reached the jetty a minute later and Marco helped her out.

'Do you know everyone in Positano?' she asked ten minutes later when they hadn't even left the beach area, continually stopped by people greeting Ben.

'Nearly.' He grinned.

He took Katya's hand as he led her up the steep stone stairs that took them past the *duomo*. Mario and Bianca had been married here with all the church trappings. He had been far away in Asia at the time but he had seen the pictures in a magazine somewhere. Mario with his arm around the woman who had been betrothed to *him*.

He tightened his grip on Katya's hand. 'Mamma's house is a bit of a climb from here, I'm afraid,' he said.

They made their way up the hill through the narrow

twisting alleys haunted by throngs of tourists. T-shirts and other items of clothing and shoes were hung on walls and placed outside shopfronts on tables. Ceramicware hung from every available surface. Artists displayed their paintings and local craftsmen hawked their jewellery in bougainvillea-draped lanes.

Bakeries and restaurants adjoined boutiques and gelaterias. Fruit and shoes and olive oil and wine and exclusive one-off dresses were sold in one vibrant clash of noise and colour. A multitude of languages and accents assaulted her ears.

Lucia was waiting for them at the front door when they'd finally made their way up the hillside.

'Somebody rang?' He laughed as he kissed both the contessa's cheeks.

'Three people,' Lucia confirmed, with a twinkle in her eye.

Ben's mother turned to Katya and clasped her hand. 'How lovely to see you again,' she said, and embraced Katya in a tight hug.

Katya closed her eyes and felt Lucia's warmth and sincerity surround her.

'Come,' Lucia said, breaking away and taking a hand each. 'Tell me why you have come to visit an old woman on such a beautiful day.'

Ben laughed at his mother's tired joke. 'We came to tell you you are going to be a grandmother.'

Lucia gasped, dropped their hands and turned, looking from one to the other. She launched herself at Ben and let loose a string of rapid-fire Italian as she kissed his cheeks repeatedly. When she was finished with Ben, she turned to Katya and rained more kisses on her, still speaking in Italian.

'Enough, Mamma,' Ben chuckled, looking at Katya's slightly bewildered look.

'Yes, yes,' Lucia said, finally pulling away, her cheeks damp with tears, and grabbing their hands again. 'Come, we'll celebrate on the terrace and we can discuss the wedding.'

Katya's step faltered and she looked over Lucia's head at Ben. He chuckled and winked at her. *Was she ready for this?*

CHAPTER SIX

A MONTH passed. Katya felt like her life was now flying along out of her control. A rather unsettling feeling for someone who had been steadfastly in the driver's seat from the age of eight. September became October, their work continued, her stomach remained stubbornly flat, but other things changed.

News of her pregnancy slowly leaked out and then snow-balled until everyone on the Amalfi coast seemed to know. Lucia, after her initial disapproval of their non-wedding plans, accepted their decision graciously and fussed round Katya like a broody hen. People regarded them as a couple. Her colleagues treated her differently. It was subtle but she definitely felt like the boss's girlfriend around the clinic.

And, the biggest change of all, she moved in with Ben. As she had promised. It was a surreal kind of life to be living, real and fake at the same time. But it was her one concession to legitimise the baby and Katya knew she would do whatever it took to instill into the collective consciousness that the baby she carried was Ben's.

They developed a routine. They would finish their theatre list for the day, spend time with their post-op cases and then Ben would take her out to dinner.

Ravello had many wonderful restaurants and she enjoyed

exploring and getting to know the charming Italian village that would be her home for the next few months.

Ben was an interesting and lively tour guide and she'd certainly never eaten so well in all her life! The locals got to know who she was very quickly and she couldn't go out of the clinic without being recognised.

After dinner they would return to the clinic and their room. And their bed. The bed that they shared. She dreaded that moment. Was even getting really good at stalling. Because climbing into that bed next to a man that would tempt a nun and then having to platonically go to sleep was an impossible task. And when she did manage to grasp the elusive tendrils of slumber, she'd dream about him. About their night together.

Was it just her stage of pregnancy? Was it just her hormones that made the images so erotic she'd wake up with a hum in her veins and a buzz deep down inside? Was it them that caused her heart to trip when she glanced at his sexy sleeping profile? Or dared her to reach out and touch him, run her finger down his cheek, so much so that her palm would tingle and she had to clamp it between her thighs to stop it from following through?

And why did she have to dream in such agonising Technicolor detail? Why was her mind blowing it up into a scene of such amazing proportions? In reality, in the grand scheme of things, it probably hadn't been that good. Really, what comparison did she have? In fact, it could have been fairly average. Probably was. She'd been a virgin after all, so what did she know?

And then she'd wake in the morning, tired and irritable, only to find a heavy male arm slung across her belly or her head snuggled into his chest and his lazy morning smile grinning down at her. Sharing a bed with Ben was a particularly exquisite form of torture.

Katya lived for the weekends when they went to the villa and had separate rooms. It was strange and lonely, the bed big and empty, but by the time Friday night came around she was just too tired to give it more than a fleeting thought.

Consequently, needing a major distraction, she threw herself into the Lucia Trust work. Every day they operated on a growing number of unfortunate patients as their work became better known. They were children mainly, some born with disfiguring deformities, others having acquired them through horrific accidents. They also did a lot of burns-related surgery, releases of contractures mainly, as well as removals of several large benign disfiguring tumours.

It was rewarding work, seeing kids with such a poor quality of life have their lot improved so dramatically. And the whole surgical team was proud of their work. Katya even started to take an interest in the behind-the-scenes work of the foundation.

Ben introduced her to Carmella Rossi, the foundation's field officer, who was infectiously exuberant about her work and explained to Katya all the ins and outs of working with myriad charities and government agencies to identify patients, and the intricacies and red tape involved with getting them to Italy.

Katya soaked it up, asking questions, even going to the control room after surgery had finished for the day. Anything, anything to take her mind off Ben and that bed.

A week later Katya found herself standing next to Ben, gowned up ready to repair a severe bilateral cleft lip and palate. She yawned behind her mask as she daydreamed about Ben's lips. The last few nights her imagination had started to embellish her dream. The Ben in her dream had told her he loved her and the Katya in the dream had confessed her love too and they'd gone on to make love again, this time even better than the first. The joining more intense, the passion even deeper.

'Katya!'

Ben's impatient exclamation cut into her fantasy. She looked at him startled, her brain taking a few more seconds to shed the heavy cloak of the fantasy and focus on the present. 'What?'

'I *said* are you ready to start?'

Above his mask Katya could only see his eyes and for a moment, as he looked at her, they were the eyes from her dreams. Deep and dark and brown, and getting darker and stormier the more he kissed her. Those incredible drugging kisses that made her lose track of time and place.

'Katya?'

She saw his eyes widen fractionally and heard the slight husky tremor in his inquisitive voice. She blinked to dispel the images in her head. 'Right, yes.' She cleared her throat. 'Okey-dokey.'

Ben chuckled at her use of slang. It seemed so strange coming in her accented English. But it was a distraction from the look he had seen in her eyes. The frank sexual hunger there was startling and he was pleased to have an operating table and a scrub top to hide his instantaneous reaction.

Sleeping in the same bed every night, her warm body and cinnamon scent temptingly close, especially when he knew what delights her body held, was becoming increasingly difficult. Even more so when he kept catching brief glimpses of that look he'd seen again just now.

Mostly she was polite and friendly but from time to time, like just now, he could see she wanted him. And, God help him, he wanted her, too. It had been months since they had made love, since she had given herself so freely and completely, and it had fuelled his every night-time fantasy since.

That look had just completely shot his concentration and he knew it didn't bode well for this morning's theatre list. Each night was an exercise in self-control. And Ben prided himself on it. She had made it clear that their cohabitation would not be sexual and he had given her assurances that he would respect her wishes. But he was just a man, just flesh and blood, and he was damned if he was going to keep his hands to himself if she kept looking at him like that.

'Good, let's start,' he said. 'Scalpel.'

The list was as frustrating as he'd thought it would be. Katya could barely meet his gaze. She seemed tired and distracted, yawning frequently. Consequently their timing was off so things took longer, and he dropped an instrument, which he'd never done before, and they couldn't get his CD to work, and the op turned out to be more involved than he'd bargained for. So the list finished later than scheduled and by the time he closed the last patient he was in a foul mood, his staff were on edge and Katya was visibly annoyed at him.

'I want to talk to you,' Ben said as they left the theatre and stripped their gowns off.

'Go to hell,' she said, dumping her gown in the linen skip.

One of the theatre nurses nearby gasped and Ben smiled, despite his mood. Only Katya would dare to tell Count Benedetto Medici, Director of the Lucia Clinic, to go to hell.

'Lovers' tiff,' he said in Italian, and shrugged dramatically as he watched Katya stride away.

He caught up with her a few minutes later as she grabbed a cup of coffee from the dining room. 'Are you OK?' he asked.

'Sure,' she said abruptly. *Nothing that a spot of sex wouldn't fix.*

Ben put a hand under her chin and noticed the dark circles under her eyes. 'You look tired.'

'That's because I *am* tired,' she said irritably, annoyed at the tingling of her skin where his fingers were resting.

Ben castigated himself. 'Why didn't you say something, *cara*? You're pregnant, for God's sake!'

'I'm pregnant Ben, not dying.'

He took the cup from her hands and gave it back to the waitress.

'Hey, I need that!' She needed something to pep her up for the afternoon list.

'No.' He shook his head. 'Caffeine is no good for the baby. You need sleep, not something that's going to keep you awake.'

'Ben—'

'Go to bed, Katya,' he ordered, placing his hand on her shoulder and priding himself on how steady his voice sounded when his mind was full of images of her going to bed. And him joining her. Kissing her neck, stroking her back. Caressing her hip.

'We have an afternoon list,' Katya said, her voice husky as he lightly massaged the muscle that sloped from her neck to her shoulder. It felt so heavenly, somewhere between asexual and erotic, and she could feel her eyes closing in response, her body swaying towards the source of pleasure.

'It will be fine, *cara*,' he murmured. She looked done in, out on her feet. Why the hell hadn't he noticed how tired she looked until now? Spending hours behind a mask every day was no excuse.

'Come on,' he said, putting an arm around her shoulders and leading her to their quarters. 'I don't want to see you in Theatre again today,' he told her as he unlocked their door and pushed her gently inside.

'Thanks, Ben,' Katya murmured.

He nodded and then shut the door and got the hell away before he was tempted to go back and join her.

Katya had a quick shower, doubting whether she'd be able to sleep with her skin still tingling, her shoulder still burning from his touch. She stepped into a towelling robe that had come with the room—the Lucia Clinic thought of everything—and pulled on a pair of knickers. She gave her hair a quick rub with a luxuriously fluffy towel. The beauty of her fine, feathery locks was that they only took thirty seconds to dry off.

Katya eyed the bed as she wandered out of the bathroom. It was exactly as they had left it that morning. Neat and tidy, the duvet smoothed of any lines. A bit like their relationship—straight and orderly. Not messy and passionate.

The thought of lying on it without Ben was strange and yet it beckoned to her, her tired brain hopeful that, without a sexy male dominating it, she might just be able to sleep. She sat on the edge and then lay back, turning on her side and tucking her knees up.

She had a fleeting moment of indecision as sleep claimed her that maybe she should change into her pyjamas in case Ben came back. But she was so tired and what if he did? The gown covered her from neck to toe. *He'd seen her naked, for crying out loud.* And, realistically, she could probably only manage a nap.

It was her last conscious thought for five hours.

Ben opened the door, ready to greet her, when he completely lost his train of thought. Katya was fast asleep on her back on the bed, a vision in white towelling. The belt at her waist had loosened and the lapels of her robe gaped slightly to reveal delicate collarbones and pale, milky skin. His eyes followed the gaping fabric, which showed a glimpse of the curve of her waist, the rise of one bony hip and the dip of her flat stomach. Her legs were almost totally exposed and he could see the scrap of white cotton hiding her modesty from him.

The whole room smelled of cinnamon. Like her. His frustrations from the day, from the last God knew how many days, all surged to the surface and he was overwhelmed by the urge to completely part the robe and just look at her. All of her.

He walked across the room to the bed, as if drawn by an invisible force, and sat on the edge. The way she looked, relaxed and peaceful, like a sated woman, made the air hard to breathe, and the room shrank until there was just him and her and the bed. His hand shook as he lifted it and hovered it over her stomach, over the place his baby was calling home.

He gave in to the urge to touch her there, cradle his baby as he had seen her do so often. He laid his hand against her flat stomach, her skin warm to touch.

Katya's eyes flew open. It took her a few seconds to break free of the clinging folds of the best, dreamless sleep she'd had in weeks. She was disorientated, momentarily confused by her surroundings.

'Ben?' Had she conjured him up?

He withdrew his hand. 'Sorry, I didn't mean to wake you.' He could see the slight rise of the inner curve of her breast, the creamy skin taunting him with its perfection.

There was an awkward silence.

Katya's head was still filled with cotton wool. 'Did you want something?'

You. Under me. Now. He couldn't think of something to say that didn't involve the damn bed.

'Ben?' Katya searched his face in the gloomy late afternoon light of the room. The heavy cloak suddenly evaporated and she was captivated by the desire in his eyes. She'd seen that look before. Still remembered the pleasure that had followed.

His brown gaze was hot. He wanted her, she could see it. She felt her own eyes widen as a flare of heat seared her pelvic-floor muscles. She felt them contract and the rub of cloth against her sensitive nipples was so excruciating she thought she might faint if he didn't soothe it with his hot, wet mouth.

He looked sexy as hell in his scrubs and her mind was full of images of how much sexier he looked out of them. She became acutely aware of her own state of undress. Nights of erotic dreams had left her ripe for this moment.

'I just came to check on you,' he said, his voice husky.

'Oh.'

Ben willed himself to move away but didn't seem to be capable of anything more vital than breathing. 'Have you been asleep all this time?'

She nodded. If he didn't get out of there soon she was going to scream. Or combust. Or demand that he make love to her.

Ben saw a blaze of desire in her blue eyes and knew his choices were running out. He should move away, leave the room, immediately. Or maybe he could just kiss her? They were hardly strangers. They'd slept in this damn bed every night for weeks. She was pregnant with his child. She looked like she wanted him to kiss her.

Just then Katya felt a quick sharp jab down low. 'Oh!' she said, fanning her hand across her stomach.

'What?' Ben asked, his brow puckering.

It happened again. Was it? Could it be? 'The baby,' she said looking up at Ben, 'it's…moving. I think I can feel it moving.' She looked at him uncertainly, the sexual haze disappearing. She was eighteen weeks gone. She'd felt the odd fluttering sensation a few times this last week, dismissed it as nothing, but this was a definite jab.

Ben's frowned slowly disappeared and a big grin split his face. 'Really? Can I feel?'

She nodded and reached for his hand, guiding it beneath hers, placing it down low. Despite the lifting of the sexually charged atmosphere, it was somehow suddenly more intimate than earlier. His heart pounded as they waited, staring at her tummy, at their linked hands.

'We scared it away,' Katya whispered. She felt strangely disappointed. The feeling had been difficult to describe. She'd felt…connected to the baby for the first time. And she'd been surprised to find herself eagerly anticipating the next one.

Ben was about to remove his hands when the baby kicked again. Katya gasped.

'There! I felt it!' he exclaimed.

Katya saw the excitement and wonder on his face and found it contagious. She smiled back at him, feeling incredibly close to the baby, like she knew it suddenly. They waited again, eager for another kick.

'I think the show's over,' Ben said a few minutes later, reluctant to remove his hand. The tiny foetal movements had been thrilling to be part of and he wished suddenly that it was he carrying their baby. To be able to play a more intimate role in their baby's development.

It was one thing feeling its first movements through his hand, but to feel it from the inside must be truly wondrous indeed. The baby had gone from being an abstract, slightly terrifying idea to being a real live little human in an instant.

Ben felt a rush of emotion rise in his chest. They were having a baby. He became aware again of his hand on her stomach. Her soft, warm skin, his hand grazing the line of her hipster knickers. He couldn't remember a time when she'd looked sexier and he wanted her even more than before. Wanted to feel her beneath him, around him. He trailed his hand up the milky path the parted robe afforded him, stopping when he reached the valley between her breasts.

He saw the desire flare in her eyes again. 'I'm going to kiss you,' he said.

Katya heard the rough texture of his voice and felt a rush of desire heat her belly and tingle between her thighs, the baby forgotten in the overwhelming urge to have his mouth against hers. Her nipples beaded again, his hand so close and her mind begged him to slip his hand beneath the fabric and touch one.

'You shouldn't,' she said quietly, her gaze flicking to his full mouth. At least her head was still grounded in reality. They really, really shouldn't. She had been adamant about the rules of their cohabitation.

'I want to,' he said as he edged closer.

'It'll complicate things.'

'You want me to, too.'

Katya swallowed, her mouth suddenly dry. Was it that obvious? She watched in fascination as he slowly lowered his head, his mouth creeping inexorably closer. 'No,' she said softly, with absolutely no conviction.

There was silence as Ben's lips inched nearer.

'I keep thinking about that night,' he said, his voice a husky whisper, his fingers sliding slowly beneath the fabric of her gown.

'So do I,' she admitted, her teeth biting into her bottom lip, her breasts aching for his touch.

'I want to look at you,' he groaned, his heart thudding as his mouth zeroed in on his goal, his fingers finding her scrunched nipple, the pad of his thumb stroking it impossibly higher.

Katya felt a moan escape her lips and arched her back involuntarily, pushing herself into his hand, moaning again when his hand cupped her entire breast. Her face flamed at her wantonness and she licked parched lips. 'I want to look at you too,' she whispered.

'Katya,' he groaned and closed the whisper distance between their mouths. The smell of her skin was intoxicating, the taste of her mouth divine. Ben groaned again, his hand tightening against her breast as he lavished her mouth with sweet, slow kisses that burned his mouth and seared his soul. He wanted to touch her, kiss her all over, know every inch of her skin, possess every inch of her body.

At the touch of his lips Katya flamed with passion, ignited by his taste and his smell and his deep erotic groans. She could feel the glide of his lips and the prickle of his stubble and the tease of his fingers at her nipple, and she opened her mouth wider, wanting to feel him deeper, closer. She lost track of time and thought, caught up in the all-consuming sensation of his mouth and his hand and their increasingly desperate kisses. She felt wanton and female and when he yanked her gown completely open she felt a surge of heat and desire pulse between her legs.

A knock on the door was a sharp intrusion into their passion and they broke off, shocked both at the interruption and at their recklessness. It was if someone had walked in and thrown a bucket of cold water all over them.

'Benedetto? Carmella is asking for you,' someone called in Italian.

Ben closed his eyes and rested his head against Katya's shoulder, sucking in air, his hand still resting on her breast, the nipple still temptingly hard. He noted with some satisfaction the harsh rise and fall of her chest and was pleased to see she was similarly affected.

'*Momento*,' he called out, and was grateful to hear the retreat of footsteps.

Katya lay very still, his hand hot against her aching flesh, struggling to come out the other side of the sexual fog and regain control of her breathing. God, what had she been thinking? This was not going to make their cohabiting any easier.

'I'd better go,' Ben said pushing away from her. He grasped the lapels of her gown and pulled them gently together, covering the temptation of her aroused breasts. He stood up reluctantly, already dismayed to see her heady sexual stare from moments ago retreating. He wanted to throw caution to the wind, forget about Carmella and stay, kiss Katya until it came back again.

Katya nodded, too aroused and shocked at her behaviour to speak. She watched him walk out the door and then rolled on her side, pulling her knees up and her gown around her to try and ease the hot, deep ache between her legs. How on earth was she going to sleep next to him now?

Ben rang an hour later to tell her he was going to be caught up for a few hours with Carmella. They were working on trying to get a patient to Italy and had run into bureaucratic red tape. He was hitting the phones, calling in favours. He was very brisk and businesslike, for which she and her still raging hormones were grateful.

Any other day Katya would have gone and helped or at least watched, but she knew it was best to be apart from him at the moment. So she ate tea with some of the live-in staff and retired back to their quarters early, pleading a headache.

She feigned interest in a book but by ten, and much to her surprise, she was falling asleep. Ben still hadn't returned and she was relieved she'd be asleep when he got back.

She was up early the next day and didn't see him until the theatre list was due to start.

'Avoiding me, Katya?' he asked in a low voice as they scrubbed up together.

'Yesterday was a mistake,' she said, paying an inordinate amount of attention to scrubbing her fingernails. 'Let's just forget it, OK?' She placed her soapy hands beneath the tap, the automatic spray clicking on and rinsing the suds away.

Forget it? How the hell was he supposed to forget it? He'd hardly slept a wink, thinking about it. The first thing he'd wanted to do when he'd arrived back at the room had been to pick up where they'd left off. Glide his hand around her stomach, pull her into him, see if he could feel the baby moving again and then take it from there. Instead, he'd turned his back to her, clamped his hands between his thighs and balanced precariously on the edge of the bed, not trusting himself to get any closer. There was no way he was going to last the next few months. No way.

Katya was conscious of Ben's weighty stare as he joined her at the table and was grateful for the routine as the first operation got under way. They had months to get through yet and Ben needed to know that one slip-up didn't mean that she was losing focus.

The first case was four-year-old Ten-ti. The child was, without a doubt, one of the cutest little girls Katya had ever seen. She had gorgeous huge brown eyes, a gappy grin and soft black hair that fell in crazy layers around her face.

She was a happy little thing, chatted away merrily at

everyone in her native tongue and had a giggle that was wickedly infectious. She had taken a particular liking to blonde-haired Katya and in the two days she'd been at the clinic Ten-ti had drawn at least a dozen pictures of her favourite nurse.

Katya had taken Ten-ti down to the garden with her that morning and the little girl had crawled into Katya's lap and laid her head against Katya's chest and waved and smiled at everyone who had come past as if to say, look at me, look how important I am.

The foundation had found Ten-ti at an orphanage. She had been abandoned at the age of one by her family when her condition had shown no signs of improving. It was hard to believe that the little girl was so happy. When Katya thought about how abandoned Ten-ti must have felt, it broke her heart. At least she wasn't going to give her baby a chance to get attached.

Katya looked down at the defect now as Ben made his first incision. The haemangioma was impressive. The vascular benign tumour protruded from Ten-ti's skull over her temple. It was quite large, about the size of a grapefruit, and its typical bright red colour was marred in the centre by a large, ugly, grey-black patch where it was badly ulcerated.

It looked like something out of a science fiction magazine. Like a maniacal cartoonist had dreamt it up—a beautiful child with a mushroom-like growth protruding from her head. A soft spongy mushroom. The nuns that ran the orphanage had been told that it would gradually get smaller and disappear, as the majority of hemangiomas did, but Ten-ti's had shown no such propensity.

At the age of four there were no signs of the tumour involuting. And the ulceration, with its associated bleeding and pain, had made her a perfect candidate for surgery.

The actual excision of the haemangioma was relatively

easy and Katya watched as Ben expertly sliced and slowly divided the tumour from the scalp. She handed him a metal kidney dish as he performed his last slice and he dropped the spongy mass into the metal receptacle.

Katya stared at it. On Ten-ti's head it had looked huge. A nasty, poisonous-looking, disfiguring mass that had isolated her and flawed her pretty features. And now, after four years of marring her life, causing her to be abandoned, it lay there, looking incongruous. Impotent. Forlorn almost.

Katya turned slightly and placed the kidney dish on her trolley, draped with sterile towels and returned her attention to the procedure. There was now a sizeable area on Ten-ti's head, about six centimetres across, where there was no skin to cover the skull.

'Closure device,' said Ben.

She had already anticipated his needs and he held out his hand at the precise time she was handing him the instrument. The transfer was seamless. No pauses or fumbling, just smooth and flawless. Textbook. A well-oiled team.

Katya had never seen these devices until now. There hadn't been much call for them in the MedSurg environment. Ben used them quite a bit and she'd even seen him use them under local anaesthetic at the bedside. They looked a bit like a fancy can-opener to her but the results were fantastic.

Ten-ti's wound was too wide for normal closure. The wound edges were too far away from each other to sew together and would normally require a skin graft. But this tricky little device was designed to stretch the skin so the margins could be brought together and then safely sutured or stapled. It worked by applying a controlled amount of tension evenly along the wound margins and exploiting the elastic properties of skin while minimising its tendency to recoil.

Ten-ti's head had been shaved around the tumour site to allow easy visualisation of the wound edges and Ben now applied the device to them. When he was satisfied with the placement he locked the device in place and started to turn the tension knob, beginning the stretching process. After twenty minutes Ben was satisfied with the approximation of the edges of the wound and he sutured it closed, using the conventional method.

'There,' he said, turning to Katya. 'She'll be as pretty as a picture.'

Katya couldn't wait to see Ten-ti's reaction when she woke up and realised that the disfiguring growth, which had bled and caused her so much pain, was no more. That was going to be a smile worth seeing.

Almost as good as the one that sparkled in Ben's eyes. His excitement and satisfaction at a job well done was palpable. He so obviously thrived on how his brainchild, the Lucia Trust, was making a real difference. She grinned back at him under her mask, struck by how different he was from the man she'd known before.

He was still as handsome, as toe-curlingly gorgeous, but at MedSurg he'd been cocky and arrogant and conceited. Overly confident. He'd matured in a few short months and she wondered about the catalyst for that. Had it just been Mario's death? She had the feeling, the more time she spent in his company, there was so much more she didn't know about him. Would never know about him.

A few hours later, Katya hurried from the theatre to visit Ten-ti. A wizened old woman with no teeth and a navy blue nun's habit smiled at Katya as she entered the room. The foundation always paid for a carer to accompany the patient and one of the nuns from the orphanage had escorted Ten-ti.

'Is she still asleep?' Katya asked, sitting on the opposite side of the bed.

'Yes,' the nun said serenely.

Katya had been surprised to find that Mi-tung had a smattering of many languages and spoke quite good English. The old nun had kind eyes and Katya was pleased that Ten-ti had known this woman's kindness.

Ten-ti stirred at the sound of Katya's voice and her eyes fluttered open. Her gaze fell on Katya, and Ten-ti gave her a weak smile. Katya smiled back and stroked the little girl's hair. There was a small dressing covering the suture line but that was all there was to remind everyone that a few hours ago a large growth had disfigured this little girl's beautiful head.

'It's amazing,' Mi-tung said in her quiet voice. 'Thank you,' she added, bowing to Katya. 'We thank you from the bottom of our hearts.'

Katya saw the old woman had tears in her eyes and felt humbled by her emotion. She reached across the bed, over Ten-ti, and held out her hand. Mi-tung didn't hesitate and took it immediately. The old woman's hand felt soft and wrinkly in Katya's and they kept their hands clasped as they watched Ten-ti sleep.

Ben found them there a few minutes later. He watched silently from the doorway for a moment. It was rare to see the softer side of Katya. She looked just like any mother sitting by her child's bedside. Concerned, dedicated.

His mind skipped back to yesterday afternoon. The memory was so vivid he could almost taste her lips, hear her moan, feel her hard, scrunched nipple against his palm.

'Here you are,' he said, deliberately interrupting his thought processes, not giving his body a chance to become any more aroused. He walked up behind Katya's chair and casually placed his hand on her shoulder. He felt her muscles tense and gently stroked her skin there so she would relax.

For a moment Katya wanted nothing more than to lean back against him and purr at his touch. But she held herself erect, very conscious of his fingers trailing a path of fire from her shoulder to her neck.

'How's she doing?' Ben asked.

'Sleepy,' Katya said, wincing at how blunt it sounded.

Ben smiled at Mi-tung and removed his obviously unwanted hand. 'I'll check back later,' he said, and withdrew.

He went to his office and shut the door. He sat behind his desk, removed his theatre cap and rubbed his hands briskly though his hat hair. He'd forgotten how infuriatingly stubborn Katya could be.

Yesterday, and on other occasions, he'd seen plainly that she'd wanted him. But right now she obviously couldn't even bear him touching her. Couldn't he even lay a hand on her without it becoming something more than it was? He drummed his fingers on the desk, frustrated beyond words.

The very last thing he wanted to do was stand beside her this afternoon and operate. Her cinnamon scent was driving him crazy, taking him right back to yesterday. To their night together. They couldn't go on like this. Something had to give.

CHAPTER SEVEN

AFTER another tense night Katya was pleased to get out of bed and away from Ben's brooding presence. She made a beeline for Ten-ti's room and was happy to find the little girl awake and sitting on the balcony with Mi-tung. For a moment the breathtaking view distracted her and she took a deep calming breath, expelling the pent-up tension caused by another platonic night.

The Mediterranean stretched into the distance, the early morning sunshine warming the cliff faces of the craggy coast-line. The gardens stepped down below in all their colourful splendour. From the nearby lemon grove she could smell a faint tang of citrus waft towards her on the light breeze.

Ten-ti lifted up her arms and Katya picked her up off Mi-tung's lap and settled with her in the other chair on the balcony. The little girl chattered excitedly and pointed to her head.

'I know, I know.' Katya laughed.

Ten-ti said something to Mi-tung and Mi-tung got up and went inside. She came back with a mirror and Ten-ti pointed at it and then at her head and stared at herself in the mirror in amazement. She angled her head from side to side and primped and preened like a teenager on a first date, and Katya laughed at her utter joy.

The little girl put the mirror down and threw herself at Katya, her little arms clinging around Katya's neck. Katya hugged her close, a lump rising in her throat. What would her child look like at four? Would he or she take after her or Ben? Would he or she have her blondeness or Ben's dark Italian looks? Would he or she ever wonder about her?

The desire to hold her own child was suddenly overwhelming and she quashed it as she squeezed Tent-ti closer. Just because she was feeling the baby move all the time now, it didn't mean anything. Other than that the baby was growing normally. Which was good. It didn't mean she was developing any motherly yearnings.

Katya felt a pang of guilt and hugged Ten-ti harder. She didn't protest and Katya was grateful, for this little girl gave her hope. Here in her arms was living proof that a child didn't need to have a mother to grow up happy and loved. It just needed someone to love it and to grow up in a loving environment.

Ten-ti justified Katya's position and Katya held onto that dearly. The last few days had been a confusing time for her with the Ben incident and the baby's first movements. There had been a lot of unexpected emotions and feelings which could threaten her plans if she allowed them free rein. Ten-ti was tangible evidence that her plan could work and Katya really needed that reassurance.

Two weeks later Ben and Katya waited in a small anteroom for Dr Rocco Gambino, the Clinic's radiologist, to finish an X-ray. It was their lunch-break and Rocco had arranged to do Katya's first ultrasound. Ben had told Katya with great pride that at one time Rocco had been one of the most experienced obstetric sonographers in the country.

Things were a little easier between them now there was some distance from the passionate kiss they'd shared. The nights were still hard but a new routine had developed. After their evening meal, Katya would go to bed and Ben would go to his office for a couple of hours and do paperwork. She would be asleep when he finally made his way back to the room and on a couple of occasions he'd even slept in his office. It wasn't perfect but at least it had taken the pressure off.

A thought that had never even occurred to Katya before, so preoccupied had she been with her plans for the baby and her attraction for Ben, popped into her head as they waited. 'What if there's something wrong with it?' she asked.

She felt a wave of dread rise over her. What if the baby was deformed or had major congenital problems? What if the fates had decided that as she didn't want the baby, she didn't deserve a healthy one? She clutched her stomach. It was still fairly flat but she could feel the bulge of her hard uterus beneath.

'It'll be fine,' Ben said.

His dismissive answer was irritating when her active imagination was already conjuring up a dozen different dire possibilities. 'Are Medici babies immune to congenital problems?' she asked.

Ben looked down into her face and saw genuine fear in her eyes. He took her hand. 'There is nothing wrong with our baby,' he said, emphasising the words carefully.

'Do you promise?' she asked.

Ben nodded. 'I promise.'

Dr Rocco Gambino came out, interrupting them, apologising for his tardiness. Ben translated as Rocco was one of the few people at the Medic clinic who wasn't bilingual. He ushered them into a cubicle and helped Katya onto the high, narrow bed.

Ben went around to the far side so he wasn't in Rocco's way. He could have easily performed the ultrasound himself but obstetric sonography was a specialised field and Rocco was the best. And, anyway, he wanted to be the father in the room, not the doctor.

Katya knew the moment the screen flickered to life and her baby appeared in a grainy black and white image that the ultrasound was the worst thing she could have agreed to. She held Ben's hand and barely heard Rocco at all. Or Ben's translation. She was totally and completely mesmerised by the tiny little life she could see on the screen.

It was no longer 'the baby' or 'it' or 'he' or 'she'. It was a real, living, breathing, kicking, squirming baby. Her baby. *All this baby needs is for you to love it*, Ben had said. And she did. Right now, her love for this tiny human being filled her completely. Overwhelmed her.

She felt connected, truly connected with her child for the first time. Feeling it kick had nothing on this. She was actually seeing inside her womb. Actually looking at her baby. It had been so easy to think of it, make decisions about it when all she'd had to confirm her pregnancy had been a pink line on a test kit and greeting the toilet bowel every morning.

But this? Actually meeting her baby. Seeing its ten fingers and ten perfect toes. Watch it as it sucked its thumb. Follow the curve of its perfectly formed spinal column. See its tiny, fragile-looking heart beat sure and steady. This was real.

Rocco pushed a button and the room filled with a magical pulsating. Whop. Whop. Whop. It was like a symphony to her ears. A concerto. There really was a baby inside her. It wasn't an abstract concept any more. An inconvenient hiccup in her life plan. It was real. She was a mother.

'Rocco says the baby is a good size and that your dates are spot on. He says everything looks fine.'

Ben could feel Katya's grip on his hand. He looked down at her, her eyes glued to the little screen. She had a strange intense expression on her face. 'He wants to know if we want to know the sex?'

Katya nodded distractedly but she hadn't really heard him. She couldn't take her eyes off her baby. She was mesmerised by the tiny central flicker in its chest.

'Katya?'

'Hmm?' she said, dragging her eyes away reluctantly from the screen. 'What?'

'Do you want to know if the baby is a boy or a girl?'

Katya blinked. Did she? She hadn't thought about it in any real sense until now. The baby's sex was just another one of those things she'd blanked out of her mind. Hadn't permitted herself to think about too much.

And if Rocco had asked her yesterday she would have given him an emphatic no. She would have classified that as information not necessary to her goal. But now, her baby on the screen in front of her, she was overwhelmed with the urge to know. 'Do you?' she asked.

Ben smiled at her sheepishly. 'I wouldn't mind,' he admitted. He had also been surprised by the power of the tiny image on the screen. Feeling the baby kicking had been amazing but this was so much more incredible. He was going to be a father and his curiosity to know everything about this tiny precious human being was incredibly strong.

Katya nodded at Rocco. He smiled at her. 'Ragazzo,' he said. 'A boy.'

A son. Katya looked back at the screen again. She was having a baby boy. She felt Ben's hand grip on hers tighten and saw his crazy grin in profile. He seemed as taken by the image as she. Would he look like his father? Would he have dark brown eyes, killer eyelashes and a quick lazy grin?

Rocco said something to Ben and Ben nodded.

'Rocco has to go,' Ben said to Katya.

No! She wasn't finished looking yet. The baby was still moving around, his tiny movements endlessly fascinating. She didn't want Rocco to switch the machine off. She wanted to watch her baby for ever.

'Katya?' Ben prompted.

Katya nodded reluctantly. She reached forward and touched her hand to the cold screen to prolong contact with her baby boy for just a little while longer. Rocco removed the transducer from her abdomen and the image went blank. She kept her hand flat against the screen, not ready to break contact. Her baby. Her son.

'There, see,' Ben teased as Katya slowly withdrew her hand, 'I told you the baby was fine.'

'He,' Katya corrected.

Ben nodded and grinned at the wonder in her voice. 'Our son.' She looked absolutely smitten. For the first time he felt a little ray of hope. Had seeing their son's image been the key to connecting Katya with her inner mother?

It had certainly helped to put things into perspective for him. He had been worrying deep down about the kind of father he would be. Bianca and Mario's betrayal had soured him to the whole meaning of love and family. And a decade of freezing them out, ignoring their pleas for reconciliation, had made him doubt whether he was capable of either.

But seeing the ultrasound had been curiously empowering. The rush of feeling that had flooded through his gut and bubbled in his veins had been too powerful to ignore. This was the meaning of love. A grainy ultrasound image blinking on a screen.

He may have been immunised against the love between a man and a woman but his heart soared knowing he was capable of a different love. The love of a father for his child.

They travelled to Ben's villa after work that night, both lost in their own thoughts. Ben watched Katya go to her room and shut the door. After the high of seeing his son today her actions were depressing. More than anything, tonight he wanted to hold her. It wasn't even about sex. He just wanted to lie beside her, pull her into him and cradle them, her and his baby. He was falling in love with the life they'd created and he wanted to share this time with her. Be as much a part of the baby growing inside her as possible.

He didn't want to be kept on the outside. He wanted to be able to touch her belly freely, feel the baby move, lay his head against her bump when they were in bed together at night. And not have to worry about her stiffening or rejecting his moves or looking at him as if he'd violated some pact.

He rustled up a fruit and cheese platter as his mind mulled over how he could achieve his goal and still keep things platonic, which was her goal. He imagined laying his head against her stomach and not wanting to make love to her and knew there was no easy middle ground.

'Katya,' he called, knocking gently on her door. 'I've fixed us something to eat.'

He heard her muffled reply and retreated to the terrace to wait for her. It was mid-November and the nights were much cooler. They wouldn't be able to stay out for long. He took a sip of some local Chianti and felt it warm him through.

'Mmm, this looks good,' Katya said, approaching from behind and plucking a slice of apple from the selection.

He smiled at her and handed her a glass of sparkling water. They indulged in some idle chit-chat, Katya asking him about the budget meeting he had attended with the foundation's financial directors that afternoon after the ultrasound. He was still wearing the suit and he looked sexy and powerful and it was taking all her willpower not to flirt. Or touch.

'The ultrasound was pretty amazing,' Ben commented lightly after a few minutes of financial talk.

Katya caught his smile and smiled back. 'Yes,' she admitted.

'Thank you,' he said. 'Thank you for letting me attend.' He knew Katya hadn't thought it necessary for him to be there.

Katya shrugged. 'It's your baby, too.'

There was a momentary silence as they both sipped at their drinks. 'I think I fell in love today,' Ben said into the quiet night air.

Katya stopped in mid-chew, startled momentarily. Her heart tripped crazily. But the look on his face put his comments into perspective. He was talking about the baby.

'You sound surprised,' she said lightly, sipping her water to cover the commotion inside.

'I didn't expect for it to be so powerful so soon.' He shrugged. 'After years of avoiding it I didn't think I'd ever feel love again in any capacity. But this just seems so…easy.'

She nodded. Her love for their baby was the one constant in her life. That and her desire to give him the best chance in life.

'You avoided love?' Katya asked, looking up at him. He was staring out over the water. Had he been hiding the real Ben behind a playboy façade?

He nodded. 'Just like you.'

He turned back and pierced her with a searching look and

Katya felt as if he'd seen inside her soul. She felt on shaky ground and needed to turn this conversation away from her. 'Someone break your heart?'

'Once.' He gave her a sad smile. 'A long time ago. I was young and stupid.'

Katya shivered at the bitterness in his last words. Someone had hurt him very badly. She felt a brief pang of sorrow for the younger Ben. It must have been awful to still be screwed up about it now.

'What about you, dear, sweet Katya? Have you ever been in love?' he asked.

'No.' Katya's answer was quick. Definite. There had been no-one in her life. She had been determined to be the exact opposite of her mother and hadn't had a moment's regret. Until one night in Ben's arms.

Ben could see the honesty in her frankness and envied her escaping the clutches of love. He'd been battered and bruised by the emotion and permanently scarred.

'Wise girl,' he muttered, and took another sip of wine.

'Until now,' she admitted, covering her tummy with her hand, the baby moving as if in agreement.

'Guess that makes two of us,' Ben said, reaching out his hand and placing it on top of hers.

Katya adjusted their placement so Ben's was snuggled close to the baby's activity. It was kicking a lot and they both stared down at her stomach and smiled at its antics.

'How can you walk away from him, Katya?' Ben asked after a minute had passed and the show seemed to be over.

Katya closed her eyes and sighed. She stood and Ben's hand dropped away. She walked over to the railing, watching the moon bathe the coast in a silvery shimmer, her back to him. She ran her hands briskly up and down her arms, the evening getting cooler as each minute passed. She had jeans and a top on but the night air had penetrated, making goose bumps on her skin and beading her nipples.

Ben rose, removing his jacket from the back of the chair. He joined her, placing it around her shoulders. Katya felt the warmth instantly and was enveloped in a snug, Ben-smelling pheromone cloud. His jacket smelled so good and she knew if she buried her face in his neck he'd smell the same, only better.

She turned to face him. It was time for honesty. He had opened up to her a little tonight and she wanted him to understand why she couldn't stay.

'When I was eleven, I was changing Leo's nappy—he was one—when my sister Sophia pulled the heater down on herself and her clothes caught light. She was very badly burned. She nearly died. To this day, she has these really horrible scars down her side and arm. Scars that I'm responsible for.'

Katya was surprised to discover tears had built in her eyes as she recounted the story. 'I'm not fit to be a mother, Ben.'

'Katya,' Ben said softly, aching for the frightened eleven-year-old he'd just caught a glimpse of. He could only begin to imagine how terrible she must have felt. '*Cara,* you were eleven years old. You were a child.'

She shook her head as a tear squeezed out and tracked down her cheek. 'I was in charge.'

Ben saw the guilt in her eyes and it clawed at his gut. He wiped the tear away gently. 'How old were your siblings when it happened?' he asked softly.

'Leo was one, Sophia was two, Marisha was three and Anna was four.' They'd all been so young. So dependent on her and she had let Sophia down.

Ben shut his eyes and dropped his forehead gently against

hers. 'Sophia's accident wasn't your fault, Katya. It was your mother's fault.'

Not according to Olgah. Katya still remembered her mother's rage when the hospital had finally tracked her down.

'I can't do it, Ben,' she said, shifting back from him slightly, his soft words very persuasive. 'I can't risk being careless and having this baby get hurt. Sometimes as I'm drifting off to sleep I hear Sophia's screams, I can smell her burnt flesh.'

Ben stroked his hand down her spine and Katya shivered. She wanted to step closer into the circle of his arms, where he was warm and male and tempting, but she had to make her point.

'I don't know how to be a good mother, Ben. I had a lousy role model and my sister nearly died because I failed in my duty of care to her. And I won't subject this baby to my inadequate mothering. I can't.'

Ben nodded. Her conviction was obvious. What had happened with Sophia had obviously had deep, long-lasting effects. She truly believed she couldn't be trusted with her own baby. Another tear trekked down her face and before he could stop himself he leaned forward and gently kissed it away.

Katya sighed and gave in to the desire to lean against him. His chest was broad and he smelled like man, like the smell that pervaded her pillow and her sheets. Suddenly the atmosphere turned sexual. The moonlight glowed on the Med to her left, stars winked down at them from above, and in front of her was a gorgeous, sexy man, holding her close. Suddenly it all seemed terribly inevitable. Fated, even.

Katya lifted her head and got a brief impression of square jaw and dark stubble and hooded eyes and then Ben's mouth was shutting it all out. His body surrounded her, pushing her back against the railings. Nearer, closer, harder. Her head spun as her senses filled with his heat and his smell and his touch.

His mouth left hers and tracked kisses down her neck and she gasped for air, her heart beating frantically. He moved with her, walking her backwards away from the terrace. Her fingers grasped his shirt for stability until a wall pressed firmly against her back. She had a vague notion he had her up against the doorjamb where the French doors separated the villa from the terrace but they could have been floating high above the Med for all she knew.

Then he was helping her out of his jacket and she was stripping off his loosened tie and unbuttoning his shirt and finally, finally laying her hands on his naked chest. His skin was hot and he moaned against her neck. The mat of hair covering his bulky pectorals trailed down his flat abdomen and felt springy and tickly against the palms of her hands. She could feel his muscles twitch and react to the path of her hands and it emboldened her to undo his belt buckle.

'Katya,' he gasped, and reclaimed her mouth as his hand trailed down from her face to claim one firm breast. She moaned and his erection surged but it wasn't enough. He was half-naked and she was still fully dressed. Her clothes looked fantastic, tight in all the right places, but he knew they'd look better crumpled in a heap on the floor. 'I want to look at you,' he groaned against her mouth.

Katya laughed. It felt good to be finally letting go, her head spinning from the pleasure rocking her body.

Ben cut off her laughter with a deep searing kiss, stripping off her top in one swift movement. Her jeans zip followed and she wriggled her hips as he pushed them down, stepping out of the denim with relative ease.

He pulled away and got his first look at her near naked body. The light from the lounge room and kitchen illuminated her body enough for him to know it was just as he remembered. Petite and feminine. Her stomach still flat despite her twenty-week pregnancy. Her skin milky. Her hips looked slightly rounder, though. And her breasts were considerably fuller. He stared at their lushness spilling out of her bra.

'Ben,' Katya begged, the look in his eyes, the roving of his gaze pure erotic torture.

'Shh,' he teased, 'I'm looking.'

Much to her amazement, Katya blushed. She had no idea why. He had seen her with fewer clothes than this. But she was conscious of her body's changes due to the pregnancy. Her hips were a little fuller and her breasts had practically exploded. She'd always been an A cup. Her breasts had been small but pert, the nipples rosy-tipped and perfectly central. But the baby had expanded them considerably and darkened the nipples to a deep dusky hue.

'You're beautiful,' he said, stroking the skin from the hollow of her throat down into her cleavage. He zeroed in on the front bra clasp and popped it, watching fascinated as her breasts sprung free. Full and lush and perky.

He noticed the prominent bluey-green veins standing out like a road map against her creamy skin. He traced the biggest one with his finger from the centre of her chest down over the swollen flesh of her left breast, to the edge of her areola. Her nipple puckered.

Katya tried to cover herself. She hated the big veins that had sprung up as her breasts had grown. 'Don't,' she said. 'They're horrible, I know.'

Ben shook his head in awe. 'No, *cara*. They are the most beautiful breasts I have ever seen. They are ready for our baby, they are all woman.'

Katya was about to protest again but he lowered his head

to a nipple and sucked it into his mouth, and she swayed against him, her knees nearly buckling at such pure sweet erotic agony. His hand covered the other breast and she closed her eyes and let her lead loll back against the doorjamb.

When he lifted his head several long drugging moments later Katya opened her eyes and gazed into his. They looked glazed, drunk with passion, and she felt heady with power. She smiled at him and he smiled back before lifting her quickly away from the doorway, hauling her up into his arms and striding through the house with her.

She revelled in the smell of his neck and the scratch of his whiskers against her nose and the way he moaned and stumbled when she licked at the pulse beating madly in his neck.

'Hurry,' she growled as she pulled his earlobe into her mouth.

Ben eased her down on the bed and stood back to admire how good she looked against his sheets. He saw the glitter in her blue eyes and noticed the uneven rise and fall of her naked breasts. He smiled and ran a finger down the centre of her chest, directly down the middle of her stomach to the edge of her undies. He continued the trek and pulled the white lacy fabric down as he went. He saw her teeth bite into her soft full lip and he didn't have to ask. She lifted her hips and he pulled the scrap of fabric all the way down.

Now she was totally naked before him and she was so beautiful and sexy he didn't know where to look, where to touch first.

'Ben!' She squirmed.

He chuckled. 'I'm just looking,' he said. 'I like to look at you.'

'What about me? Maybe I like to look at you, too.'

Ben grinned. 'Your wish is my command.' And he quickly stripped off his half-undone trousers and followed them with his designer jocks. His erection sprang free and it felt good to have no constraints.

Katya had thought she'd had him fairly represented in her

dreams, that her imagination had conjured him up perfectly. But looking at him now, the fantasy paled in comparison. Ben was all male. Every hard, strong, Italian inch of him.

She reached her arms up and almost fainted from pleasure when he covered her body with his solid male frame. 'Yes,' she whispered just before he kissed her.

Their passion ignited. His kisses grew hotter, longer deeper. His mouth left hers and found a nipple and she bucked against him like a bolt of electricity had coursed through her. She whimpered as he created pleasure and pain in equal parts. 'Please, Ben,' she begged, grinding her hips against his.

He chuckled and looked up at her from her wet nipple. 'No, Katya. I want this to be slower this time. Like I should have done it last time. Like I would have if I'd known you were a virgin.'

Katya gave a frustrated growl. 'My virginity is gone. Get over it.'

Ben laughed at the appearance of blunt Katya but his eyes widened as he saw a fierce light burn in her eyes.

'If I don't feel you inside me now, I'm going to scream.'

'Katya, *cara*,' he said soothingly,' I want to make sure you are ready.'

Katya laughed. 'Oh, God, Ben. I am, trust me. Can't you tell?'

He could. His senses swam with a heady mix of cinnamon and aroused woman. Ben saw the desperation, the sexual frustration glittering in her eyes. She was lifting her hips and his erection was rubbing against her hot moist core. He held her gaze as he trailed two fingers down her stomach. They continued through the downy hair and teased her slick entrance.

A wave of heat surged through his body at her readiness, almost blinding him with intensity. 'Katya,' he groaned.

'Ben, please,' she whispered, her voice hoarse with need. 'I promise after this you can impress me with your tricks but, please, I need you in me now!'

Katya lifted her hips, trying to catch his erection and guide him inside. 'Please, Ben,' she begged.

'Katya,' he groaned lowering his head to kiss her as he gave in to his base urge and hers and entered her tight, hot core.

'Yes,' she said. 'More.'

'Katya,' he moaned, again, moving inside her beyond any semblance of control.

Katya had been hot and ready for this for weeks. Nights fuelled by erotic dreams had primed her for this moment and it took only a few strokes of his rock-hard erection to tease the sensitive flesh into blast-off. 'Ben. Oh, God, I can't hold this back…it's too…much,' she panted, enjoying the build-up as it undulated through her internal muscles.

Ben knew the feeling. Katya's readiness, her eagerness and erotic dreams of his own were powerful catalysts. He could feel her trembling under him. He could feel her tighten around him further and he knew that as she let go and her muscles milked him that in a few more strokes he would join her.

She was raking her nails down his back as his orgasm erupted. His muscles tensed, his breathing stopped, his heart skipped a beat for a few seconds and then it came and he pounded into her again and again, urged on by her cries and his powerful, all-encompassing release.

And somewhere, up there, while she was out of her body, shattering into a thousand pieces, Katya realised the awful truth. That she had fallen in love with Ben. That she was no better than her mother. She'd thought she was above such emotions, immune after years of her mother's dramas but ultimately the old adage, like mother like daughter, had proven true.

She had fallen for someone who couldn't love her back.

* * *

Katya woke a little later to find Ben staring down at her. He was tracing the veins on her breast again and she realised her nipples had been responding even in her sleep. He gave her a lazy smile and a surge of love welled up in her chest.

'I love these,' he said quietly, following a green pathway. 'I love them because I know they're making you ready to nurture our child. Are you sure you won't reconsider?' His hand moved lower, to her stomach, and he cradled it.

Katya looked at him and knew it was more important than ever now to leave. She had done the dumbest thing on earth, fallen for a man who didn't believe in love. So that was two reasons she couldn't stay. The baby and being with someone who couldn't—wouldn't—ever love her back.

Her life stretched before her, a long lonely corridor of time. She felt a tear escape. Katya closed her eyes as Ben dipped his head to kiss it away as he had done earlier. He was gentle and reverent and she thought her heart would burst it ached with so much love for him. His hand felt heavy and warm on her stomach and she felt completely possessed.

Surprisingly the thought didn't fill her with dread or revulsion. My how things had changed! She had been resisting a man's ownership for years but now she was here, she knew her life would never be the same. Was this how her mother had felt with each of her men? For the first time in a long time Katya felt a strange link with the woman who had given her life.

Ben pulled her in close, spoon-fashion, one hand cupping her stomach. One tear became two, became three until she was crying a river in the bed. Ben hushed her and kissed her hair and she cried even more. It felt like heaven to be safe in his arms and he held her till she fell asleep.

CHAPTER EIGHT

BEN and Katya spent the weekend in bed. In fact, they spent a lot of their weekends in bed over the following months. Either in their villa or on *The Mermaid*. By some kind of unspoken agreement, they both knew denying themselves was stupid. They didn't question it, they didn't even speak about it, they just let it happen.

Katya was surprised at how easy it was. How easy Ben made it. Loving him and knowing that he wouldn't love her back hurt. But walking away now wouldn't help her love him any less. She still had a goal—the baby. And she had to finish what she had set out to do.

So, was there something wrong with having a few brief months where the eight-year-old Katya's romantic fairytale played out? Was it wrong to make the most of her time with Ben and just enjoy it? Life without him, without her son would go on. It would be hard, her heart would be well and truly broken, but she knew she was strong enough to do it. Was it wrong to want this for a little while?

Still, living in the lap of luxury was hard to get used to. Years of being poor and living frugally were harder than she'd imagined to overcome. She was enjoying the perks but the wealthy mindset that was inherent in Ben was still a foreign concept to her. She kept thinking she'd do or say something to embarrass him, show her lack of breeding. And despite his inclusion of her in every part of his life, she felt like an interloper, like Cinderella waiting for the clock to strike twelve.

Ben was great. He took her out and showed her all around the Amalfi coast. To Priano, Minori and Sorrento. He took her over to Capri on his boat, to the Blue Grotto and the Emerald Grotto. And one memorable afternoon he drove her to see the ruins at Pompeii. They dined with his mother and Katya loved going to Positano for their visits. Of all the places he'd taken her, she loved Positano best.

He took her to fabulous restaurants, way off the beaten track, where the tourists didn't go. She ate amazing dishes, like Parmigiana Melanzane and mussels caught fresh from the Med cooked in wine, lemon juice and pepper. And bruschetta. Katya developed a real craving for bruschetta.

But it had to be Taddeo's. Taddeo owned a restaurant not far from Ben's villa and they often ended up there for Katya's favourite food. Taddeo had told her the first time he'd served it up to her, 'When you go home tonight, *bella*, you will dream of my bruschetta.' She had laughed but he had been dead right. It was divine with just the right blend of basil and onion and the final touch—a drizzle of olive oil. And she had asked for seconds and had made Taddeo's day.

The weeks flew by. Christmas and New Year passed. Her belly grew into a decent-sized bump. Ben loved watching her grow with his child—her stomach expand, her breasts flower. He rejoiced in every kick, every somersault. Every day that passed he fell further in love with his son. And Katya fell further in love with him.

Work was great as well. They worked well together, probably better now sexual frustration wasn't making them edgy and tense. And Katya was surprised every day by how much she loved the work. It was so different to the madness of the frantic get-them-in, get-them-out world of MedSurg. At the Lucia Clinic there was time to follow a patient through, to get involved.

And that surprised her, too. The MedSurg environment had suited her emotional state for many years. The insanity of war and senseless violence became blunted in the frantic atmosphere, but as her pregnancy advanced and her hormones bloomed and she fell deeper in love with Ben, the emotional involvement the clinic afforded her gave her job satisfaction she'd never dreamed of. The old Katya would have scoffed at such human sentiment, shied away from it even, but she was softer these days.

Was it love or the baby? She suspected a bit of both. One thing was for sure, she had a lot to thank Ben for. If she'd never fallen pregnant and never come to Italy, she would never have known this other side of herself existed. Never known she could be this…female. Sure, she'd always looked like a woman, but perhaps now she was thinking and feeling more like one.

She was even developing an understanding of her mother. Maybe they'd never be close but Katya was starting to appreciate that sometimes things weren't so black and white. She could see her mother's choices through the eyes of a woman now, instead of those of a child. How love and duty for your child could war with the love you could feel for a man. Did that excuse her mother's neglect? No. Did it make it a little more comprehensible? Yes.

She was thirty weeks before she knew it. Her bump was soccer-ball-sized now. And she was tired. A lot. And her feet had started to swell at the end of each day from standing for hours and hours at an operating table. Ben would massage her feet each night and tried to persuade her to finish work early. But Katya refused.

Working with Ben was the one thing that helped keep their relationship in perspective. It gave it a professional aspect that she needed to keep from surrendering her heart completely. It gave her a different view of Ben for eight hours a day. Ben the surgeon. Not Ben the father of her baby. Or Ben her lover.

It was a daily dose of reality and she didn't want to lose that sitting at home all day waiting for Ben, the man that she loved, to come home from work. That definitely smacked too much of happy families and she was determined to keep working until the day she went into labour.

But in her thirty-first week, the baby pulled rank. Followed closely by Ben.

'Are you OK?' he asked her quietly at the end of a particularly long day. Ben had noticed her rocking on her heels quite a lot throughout the long operation and moving from foot to foot.

He was repairing a severe burns contracture of the face and neck. The ten-year-old boy had sustained his initial injury through a kerosene explosion several months before and inadequate treatment had led to the current grotesque disfigurement.

The contractures involved the eyelids, face, neck and chest, the resulting downward pull leading to the boy's inability to shut his eyes or mouth. There was a fixed flexion deformity of the neck so that his chin was sitting against his chest, with the front of his neck not visible at all. Looking at the poor boy it was as if his skin had melted from his face and fused his head to his chest.

So it was a big repair job, involving skin grafting and complicated by difficulty gaining and maintaining anaesthesia. Four hours in, Katya's back ached, her legs ached, she was starving and feeling exceedingly light-headed.

'I'm fine,' she dismissed, knowing that they were on the downhill run and she could sit and eat something very soon.

They were stripping off their gowns fifteen minutes later, Ben chatting away excitedly about the op. He'd done a fantastic job and given a little boy back his face and neck. Katya could hear him vaguely, her rebelling stomach and a surge of nausea distracting her from his words.

Her ears started to ring and then she couldn't hear him at all. She could see his mouth moving but the words were lost in the noise coming from inside her head. Her vision started to go next. Ben was shrinking before her eyes as a black fuzz slowly encroached on her field of sight. And then everything went black and she fell.

'Katya? Katya!' Ben caught her as she slumped against him. He gave her a shake and she flopped like a rag doll. He swore in Italian and swept her up into his arms. He strode down the corridor, past surprised staff, getting angrier with each footstep. He kicked the door to his office open and laid her down on the double sofa.

She murmured and he let out a pent-up breath, his heart hammering madly. 'Katya?' he said again.

Her eyes fluttered open and he was so relieved for a moment he wanted to kiss her instead of strangle her.

'What happened?' she asked, half sitting.

'You fainted.' He pulled a blood-pressure cuff out of a desk drawer, wrapped it around her arm and took a quick reading.

'Eighty over thirty-five,' he told her disgustedly.

Katya returned his told-you-so look with a baleful glare. 'My blood sugar got a little low,' she said, ripping the cuff off and sitting up. Her head swam for minute and she shut her eyes briefly, willing it to stop.

When she opened them Ben was looking at her with raised eyebrows. 'What?' she said crankily. 'Pregnant women faint from time to time.'

Ben swore again in his native tongue. She'd scared the hell out of him. 'I will not have you jeopardising this baby's health because you want to be some kind of super-nurse.'

Ben's blunt reminder that to him she was just a life-support system for their baby stung. But it was a good reminder to her foolish heart of her purpose here in Italy, which seemed to get more and more blurred the longer she stayed.

'I am not giving up work,' she said stubbornly.

'Oh, yes, you are,' he countered, rising from his crouched position to sit behind his desk.

'You think if you sit behind that desk that it makes you more important? That I'll suddenly realise you're the count and I'm the commoner and I'll bow before you?'

Ben chuckled. Hardly! Katya was not like any other woman he'd ever known. Fawning and flattery just weren't part of her persona. She had her own opinions and spoke her own mind. She'd certainly been a refreshing change from all the others.

'Would you?'

'Not a chance.'

Ben chuckled again. It was good to see a glimpse of her prickliness. She had lost a lot of that edge to her personality over the weeks and it was reassuring to still see flashes of her old spark. The Katya who had never given him an inch.

Too many women had hung on his every word once upon a time and he'd soaked it up. Even Bianca had been a major ego trip for him. Being with someone who afforded him no such adulation had made him see that about himself. In fact, Katya made him work for his compliments and he was surprised at how much more rewarding it was.

A knock on the door interrupted them. It opened to reveal Carmella. 'I'm sorry,' she said, looking from one to the other, 'I'm interrupting something?'

'Yes,' Ben said.

'No,' Katya said, glaring at Ben.

'Katya's giving up work,' he told Carmella.

'No, Katya's not,' Katya denied hotly.

Carmella looked from one to the other, as if she was watching a tennis match. 'Right…maybe I should come back later,' she said, backing out the door.

'No,' Katya said. 'Go ahead. Ignore me.' She lay back on the lounge. In truth, she'd have liked to have risen from the couch and stalked out of the room with her head held high, but she still felt a little dizzy.

Ben and Carmella slipped into Italian and Katya let it swirl around her as she shut her eyes and waited to feel more grounded. She heard papers rustling and realised that she kept hearing a word she was familiar with. Mulgahti.

She sat up. 'What are you talking about?' she asked.

Ben and Carmella stopped what they were doing and turned to her. 'There's a baby girl in a remote village that has been brought to our attention, but her extraction is proving difficult due to internal politics.'

'Mulgahti?' Katya asked. 'That's the village?'

Ben frowned. 'Yes. Do you know it?'

Katya nodded and rose. A wave of dizziness swept over her and she swayed momentarily. Ben stood and was at her side in an instant. 'Katya!' Exasperation laced his voice.

She leaned against him briefly. 'I'm fine,' she mumbled,

pushing away from him and walking on shaky legs to the desk. Carmella offered Katya the chair she'd been sitting in and Katya felt too weak to refuse.

'I was stationed not far from Mulgahti a few years ago,' she said, locating it easily on the map that had been spread on the table. 'MedSurg spent six months there, treating victims of the local civil war.'

Carmella glanced at Ben. 'Do you have any contacts there still?' she asked Katya.

Katya thought for a moment. It was a difficult area, controlled by local warlords, one of whom they'd patched up after he'd taken a bullet to the shoulder. 'Maybe,' she said. 'Gill would be the best contact. I can make a few phone calls.' She looked first at Carmella then at Ben.

Carmella looked at Ben then back at Katya. 'Any help you can give would be welcome,' Carmella said.

Ben saw the smile that Katya gave his field officer and the spark of interest in Katya's eyes, and an idea started to form in his head. 'Why don't you two stay here in my office and see what progress you can make?' he suggested. 'Carmella can help you with any information you might need,' he said to Katya.

Katya nodded, feeling a tremor of excitement course through her, knowing she might be able to help get a child in need of medical attention to the Lucia Clinic. 'It's the middle of the night in Australia—Gill's not going to be happy.'

She grinned at Ben and he grinned back. 'He'll be fine when he realises why you're ringing.'

Katya nodded and picked up the phone.

'Can I get you ladies something?' he asked.

'Food,' Katya said, dialling the number.

He chuckled. 'Anything in particular?'

She shook her blonde head. 'As long as it's fast. I'm starving.'

Ben returned fifteen minutes later with a plate laden with bruschetta. Carmella was sitting in his seat, talking into her mobile in Italian and Katya was sitting where he'd left her, speaking in Russian. He plonked the plate on the table between them and they both automatically reached for a piece while they continued their conversations.

He placed his hands on Katya's shoulders and lowered his head to whisper in her ear. 'I'm sorry its not Taddeo's.'

Katya turned her head and smiled at him, still talking in rapid Russian. He stood and massaged her neck for a few moments. He smiled as she relaxed back against him. He could see the rise of her burgeoning belly from this vantage point and he just wanted to let his hands slide down her front and link them together under her bump.

Katya dropped her head to one side and he concentrated on the exposed muscles of her neck. He realised suddenly that he could also see down her scrub top to her lace-covered, full, ripe breasts, and he wished Carmella was somewhere else. He pictured cupping them, kneading them as he was her neck, until the nipples peaked in his hands. Spinning her around in the swivel chair, lifting her top and tasting them.

A knock interrupted his fantasy.

'Here you are. Benedetto. We're waiting for you,' Gabriella reprimanded in Italian.

Ben looked at his watch. He'd lost track of the time completely. 'Sorry. I'll be right there,' he said.

He dropped a kiss on Katya's shoulder, where the scrub top gaped and exposed the creamy skin.

'Later,' he murmured.

They were sitting on their terrace that evening, enjoying a candle-lit dinner. Katya was excitedly relaying how she and

Carmella had successfully managed to organise safe passage for the Mulgahti patient. The baby girl would be at the Lucia Clinic in two days.

'Carmella is very busy. She's been complaining for a while that she needs another staff member,' Ben said, keeping his voice very matter-of-fact.

Katya stopped in mid-chew. 'Ben…' she said, a slight warning in her voice.

'Katya, it's perfect.'

'I don't want to give up work,' she said.

'You won't be. You'll still be working. But you'll get to sit instead of standing on your feet for hours. You'll be able to eat regularly and take regular breaks.'

Katya looked at him, the candlelight throwing warm shadows on his dark features. He made the offer very attractive. Being on her feet all day was more tiring then she'd ever admit to him or even herself. Plus she'd be out of Ben's company, too, which would be an easier transition for her when she had to leave in another couple of months. It was time she started withdrawing a little. But what if she missed being a scrub nurse?

Ben could see her wavering. 'Look, just think about it for a few days, OK?' He reached across and placed his hand over hers.

She looked at him and smiled. 'OK, I'll think about it.'

He grinned triumphantly and she shook her head at him and rolled her eyes and returned her concentration to the food in front of her. Now that she had told Ben all about her day, her thoughts returned to something that Carmella had said at one stage. It stewed away in her brain as she ate some of Taddeo's gnocchi.

Ben noticed her getting quieter. 'Penny for them,' he said.

Katya looked at him, startled. She toyed with her food and eventually took a bite. 'It's nothing,' she said, shrugging her shoulders.

'Katya,' he said gently, 'you can tell me anything.'

Katya wasn't so sure about that. But he looked like he believed it anyway. She took a deep breath. 'I was just thinking about the girl who broke your heart. You never talk about her. Or Mario.'

Ben swallowed his mouthful of food, surprisingly without choking. This was not what he'd been expecting. 'It was a long time ago,' he said abruptly.

Just as she'd thought. She felt a nagging sense of regret that Ben didn't think he could talk to her about his feelings over his brother's death and the mystery woman who had broken his heart. He knew all her secrets now, all about her dirt-poor background, her mother's neglect and the incident with Sophia. Surely he should be able to tell the woman he made love to every night some of his past too?

'Mario's death wasn't.'

'Katya.'

She held up her hand. 'Carmella commented today that this was the happiest she'd seen you since Bianca. I didn't even know that was her name. I guess I suddenly realised that I don't know much about you. Your past, your secrets. It seems odd to be…' Katya chose her words carefully '…living with you and not know you.'

'You know me.'

Katya shook her head, the candle flame dancing in the light breeze. 'I know the man you were when we were with MedSurg is very different to the man you are here, in Italy. I mean…you are the man you are today because of the things that have happened in your past.' *You can't love me because of her.* 'I'd just like to be able to understand, that's all.'

Ben could see her sincerity. She wasn't asking out of some ghoulish curiosity, she genuinely wanted to understand what made him tick. He sighed. 'It's hard for me to talk about Bianca. Or Mario. I was angry for so long. And proud. And then they died. And I was ashamed that I had rejected any attempts at reconciliation. Mario had tried. Bianca had tried. Mamma had tried.'

Katya frowned. So Bianca had died, too? She was confused. Were his ex and his brother not two separate issues? 'I'm sorry,' Katya said. 'Bianca is dead, too? Were their deaths linked?'

Ben gave a bitter laugh. 'You could say that.' He saw her puzzled look and stopped being cryptic. He was so used to everyone knowing, he'd forgotten that she didn't. 'Bianca and I were engaged to be married. I was totally besotted with her. I was twenty-four…young, foolish. I found her and my brother together, in the clinic gardens. They were kissing. He had his hands on her…she was half-naked. That's when I left Italy. I ran away as far as I could go and Bianca and Mario got married.'

'Oh, Ben, how awful.' Katya heard the emotion in his voice. She could only imagine how devastating such a betrayal must have been. Now she understood the estrangement Ben had talked about. Now she could see why he was sworn off love. He was obviously in no hurry to risk his heart again after it had been battered so soundly.

Katya, better than anyone, understood how things like that could affect you for ever. And she knew that any hope she was harbouring that Ben might grow to love her would never come to fruition.

'The irony is Mario and I were so close until then. Oh, we were rivals. In everything. We were always trying to best each other with the biggest and the best, the latest and the greatest. But it was good-natured. He was my older brother, there was only twelve months between us, I hero-worshipped him and our rivalry pushed me to be the best I could be. But he took our one-upmanship too far when he took Bianca.'

Oh, dear, Katya thought. It seemed they'd both been victims of their idols developing feet of clay. Ben had just been much older before life had turned on him.

'Did you ever speak to each other again?' she asked.

Ben shook his head. 'He tried to extend an olive branch. They both did.'

'Bianca was in the car crash with your brother?'

Ben nodded. 'I may not have respected him, may have wanted nothing to do with him, but I didn't wish him dead. Either of them.'

Katya could see the truth of his words written all over his face. He was looking at her earnestly, his eyes begging her to understand. And she did. As much as she disliked and didn't respect her mother, Katya knew she would be devastated when the inevitable happened. No matter what, Olgah was the woman who had given her life.

'It's funny how a decade of hostility and self-righteousness can suddenly seem so churlish,' he said quietly, mesmerised by the flame.

Guilt. Another emotion Katya knew intimately. 'It sounds to me like they didn't do it to hurt you, Ben. Maybe they just fell in love? It happens sometimes. They say forgiveness is good for the soul.'

Deep down he knew he needed to be able to forgive them. But the image of Mario and Bianca in the garden was etched into his memory. And after years of it, absolution was a big thing to ask. 'Like you've forgiven yourself?' he said, fixing her with a hard stare. 'Forgiven your mother?'

Katya felt his accusation hit her in the solar plexus and

blinked at the sudden turn in the conversation. It struck even harder because she knew he was right.

Ben saw her eyes widen and immediately castigated himself. 'I'm sorry,' he said. 'That was uncalled-for.' He rubbed his hands through his hair. 'This topic drives me crazy.'

'Because it's unresolved?'

'Because Mario and Bianca are everywhere I go here. At the clinic, at Mamma's, in the streets of Positano, in the piazza at Ravello. I bought this villa so I could get away from memories of them. This is my sanctuary from the past. Coming back to Italy to fulfil my family duty has been made so much harder because of all the memories. And everything I do here has Mario's stamp on it. All of it makes me crazy.'

Katya nodded. It must be hard for such a proud man to have to continually face ghosts from an incident that had driven a wedge through his family for a decade. 'Maybe it's time to make some new memories?' she suggested.

He looked at her and realised suddenly that, thanks to her, he had a whole host of new memories. Very, very pleasant ones at that. And with the advent of the baby, his son, even more to come.

He nodded. 'Hence the clinic,' he said. 'Coming back from MedSurg and the poverty-stricken countries I've worked in, the opulence and the luxury here seemed so disproportionate. And I kept hearing your voice, nagging in my head, about hedonistic pampered rich people.'

Katya smiled. 'Nice to know you thought about me.'

'Oh, I thought about you,' he said, and chuckled as Katya blushed. 'Getting the Lucia Trust up and running and finding someone else to take over the management of the rest of the clinic has given me something to focus on that's truly mine. I've been able to blend the old direction with a new one and put my own stamp on it. Made it something other than a vanity clinic for the rich and famous. Made it mine. And I'm proud of that.'

'As you should be,' Katya murmured.

Her quiet confirmation meant more than any effusive display. He could tell from her earlier excitement and her involvement with their clients that the clinic had come to mean a lot to her as well. That she was also proud of the work they were doing with the foundation. He was surprised to find that it mattered to him. What she thought of him.

'But then I go into the gardens and I see Mario everywhere. He loved those gardens. Every nook and cranny reminds me of that day…rounding a corner to see Bianca with Mario…her shirt unbuttoned…'

Katya felt sick at the dread in his voice. He may say he had sworn off love but he must still be in love with Bianca if a decade later he couldn't even bear to say the words. Was he still in love with her? A dead woman? Who'd betrayed him? Something squeezed her heart and the hopelessness of her love was brought into sharp focus.

'Are you angrier with him or with her?' she asked.

Ben blinked. No one had asked him that before. And if they had, he probably would have said Bianca. But being forced to confront it now, he realised he was angriest with his brother.

He sighed. 'Mario, I guess. There are just some lines you don't cross.' It felt amazingly cathartic just to admit it.

Katya nodded. She understood a little better now that people were only human, with human failings. 'Of course, Ben, he was your brother. You idolised him. And he let you down. And then you had to go from hating him to grieving him with no time in the middle for reconciliation. But you can't get over it by denying he ever existed. Running away from the memories. You need to be able to accept he was human and celebrate his life.'

Ben frowned. 'What do you mean?'

She shrugged. 'I don't know.' She groped around for an idea. 'How about some kind of memorial for him and Bianca in the gardens somewhere? Put your own stamp on them, too?'

Ben regarded her seriously and nodded slowly. 'Maybe.' He was beginning to think that Mario and Bianca had done him a favour. Had they never betrayed him, he wouldn't have ever known Katya. And suddenly he couldn't imagine being without her.

CHAPTER NINE

A WEEK later Katya stopped midway up the clinic's grand stone staircase for a breather. It had been long day in the operating theatre and everything ached. Ben's offer to move her into the administration side with Carmella was looking more and more attractive as standing for long periods of times was becoming very wearying.

She looked down at her belly and wondered how it could possibly get any bigger. And she still had eight weeks to go! The baby seemed to have had a growth spurt and she felt uncomfortable and was sure she was waddling. Ben reassured her that she wasn't, which was sweet, but she knew he was lying.

Katya had never known it was possible to be this tired. The baby's size was even making it uncomfortable to sleep so she was back to being an insomniac again.

'You OK?' Ben asked, coming up behind her. One hand automatically reached for the muscles at her neck and started to knead them. The other automatically caressed the bulge of her tummy. He dropped a kiss against her neck.

'A few months ago I could take these stairs two at a time.' She grimaced, closing her eyes as his fingers worked their magic.

Ben could see Katya was looking more and more exhausted each day. '*Cara,*' he said softly, 'I think it's time to give up work.'

Katya's eyes flew open and she stepped away from him. 'I'm fine,' she said testily.

'*Cara,*' he said, looking at her reprovingly.

'What happened to working with Carmella?' she asked.

'I think it's becoming obvious that you just need to put your feet up and rest.'

And sit around thinking about you all day? She shook her head. 'No. I like working. I like working here particularly. Don't you understand? I didn't expect to but I do. If I sat around doing nothing all day I'd go mad.'

God, she could be exasperating. 'Katya, think of the baby.'

She heard the reproach in his voice and wanted to kick him in the shins. *Well, as long as the baby's OK.* 'The baby is fine,' she said, and turned on her heel.

Except somewhere in the execution of her about-face she tripped herself up and before she knew it she'd slipped and fallen and was bumping down the stairs, flailing around like a beached whale, trying to stop, trying to protect the baby from the fall.

'Katya!' Ben lunged for her but couldn't grab her in time and he rushed down the stairs, reaching her as she came to a stop in a crumpled heap at the bottom.

'Katya. Katya!' His heart was galloping in his chest. 'Are you all right?' She was lying very still and he turned her over, a dozen dreadful scenarios marching through his brain. God, please, let her be all right!

Katya's eyes fluttered open. She moaned. Now she really did ache everywhere. Her arms and legs felt battered and she lifted her hand to the back of her head and gingerly prodded a rapidly growing lump.

'What?' Ben investigated the bump. 'I think you need an X-ray.'

Like hell. She wasn't exposing her baby to any unnecessary radiation. '*I*'m fine, Ben,' she protested weakly, pushing herself up.

'No, we need to get you checked out,' he said, supporting her into a sitting position.

Katya looked into his eyes. She could see the concern in his brown gaze. Was it for her or for the baby? 'The baby's fine,' she said, and stood up, shaking his hands off her.

'The bump on your head needs looking at. You took a big tumble.'

'I feel fine,' she said again, pushing away from him feeling irritated by his concern.

Ben watched her go and raised his eyes heavenward. *Give me strength!* If she thought he was just going to let her walk away and not get checked out then she didn't know him at all.

Katya hurried away, knowing she was being unreasonable, but loving him and knowing that his only interest in her was the baby and some latent sexual chemistry was harder than she'd thought.

She felt a sudden warmth between her legs and stopped abruptly, looking down. 'Ben!'

His eyes flew open and he ran to her side as she stood stock-still in the corridor, her hand clutching her stomach.

'I'm bleeding,' she said, staring at the growing red stain on her scrub pants and then looking at him. The baby. Had she hurt the baby?

Ben felt his heart in his mouth when he saw her blood-stained clothes. He swore and swept her up into his arms.

'Where are we going?' she asked, clinging to him, trembling all over, biting her lip to stop the tears that were building in her eyes.

'Rocco.'

Katya lay very still as Rocco ran the transducer over her belly. Her mind was frozen, fear for her baby bringing up all the horrible possibilities. How could she have been so stupid? Why had she insisted on working? If she'd been sitting at home with her feet up, this would never have happened. *I'm sorry, baby, I won't put you in danger again.*

Ben and Rocco were talking in Italian over her, pointing at various things on the screen, but she wasn't listening. Her eyes were fixed on the image. At the baby's strong heartbeat and its vigorous, healthy movements.

He was OK. The baby was OK. Her relief was immense. As was the sudden clarity that descended on her. She could no more hand her son over to Ben than fly to the moon. She touched the screen as she had done at her first ultrasound. *I promise to protect you from everything. I promise to be vigilant. I promise to give you everything I have. I promise to love you above all else.*

'Rocco says the baby looks good. The fall seems to have caused a small area of the placenta at the margin to come away and bleed. But the rest of the placenta looks healthy.'

Katya nodded, a surge of relief bringing her thought processes back on line. 'Thank you,' she said to Rocco.

'As the bleeding's now stopped Rocco recommends bed rest for a couple of days and then he'll scan you again. But if you notice any decrease in foetal movements or any more bleeding, he wants to see you straight away.'

'Of course,' Katya said eagerly. She would have lain in bed for the duration if that's what it took for the baby to be OK.

Rocco left and Katya sat on the narrow couch, letting Ben do a full neuro assessment on her. It was making him feel better and she was still so relieved to see the baby was OK, she didn't even think to protest. After it was done he walked her up to their quarters, stood outside the cubicle while she showered and then tucked her into their bed.

'Do you want me to stay?' Ben asked. It had been a frightening couple of hours and the last thing he wanted to do was go back to work. But there was still one more case to complete.

'No.' Katya smiled reassuringly, lying on her side and hugging her belly. 'I'll be fine.'

'Page me if you need me,' he said, dragging the bedside phone closer to her. 'I'll bring us some dinner when I finish.'

Katya nodded and was grateful when Ben finally left. Her mind was whirring around despite the classical music that Ben had switched on before he'd left. She knew what she had to do. She couldn't stay any longer.

She knew now there was no way possible she could hand this baby over to Ben and walk out of its life. Those awful moments when she'd thought she was losing the baby or had harmed the baby had been the worst of her life. Worse than discovering her pregnancy. Worse than admitting her love for Ben. Why had it taken a threat to the baby's life for her to realise the truth? It was her destiny to be a mother to this child.

What kind of a fool had she been? Yes, she had been scared. Scared that she'd make a mess of it. Scared that something awful would happen to him as it had happened to Sophia, as it nearly had today. Scared that she couldn't provide for him like Ben could. Scared of the single-parent life she was about to embark on which her own mother had failed at so miserably.

But all that paled in comparison to her love and desire to be with this baby. Ben's son. Her fear of never seeing her child far outstripped her fear of failure. She was just going to have to be the best damn mother she could. The safest. The most vigilant. The most loving. Because she'd known, looking at that screen, her baby strong despite the trauma it had been through, that she couldn't give her baby up. She'd known it as surely as she'd known that day that she couldn't terminate the pregnancy.

The revelation had been unexpected. It had been much simpler before today. Pregnant with baby. Don't want baby. Have baby. Leave baby with father. Simple. Straightforward. Uncomplicated. Although as each day passed and the end drew nearer and she felt a deeper and deeper connection with the baby, the lines were blurring. And falling in love with Ben had complicated it further.

And now things were as sticky and mired and complicated as they could get. And that meant only one thing. She had to get out. Leave Ravello. Leave Positano. Leave Italy. Leave Ben. Get as far away as possible. Because she couldn't hand her son over and she couldn't stay either. Ben had made it very clear that he wouldn't love again. Couldn't love again. And she couldn't live with him, loving him, knowing that she'd never hear those words.

Sitting in their house, waiting for him to say them, hanging on, getting more and more desperate every day—like her mother. Becoming old and bitter, like her mother? Seeing him heap love on their child. Growing jealous of that? No, she would slowly wither and die. There was no choice. She had to cut her losses now.

Loving Ben these past few weeks had been a surprise and a complication she could have done without but she was a big girl, a practical woman, and she'd known she could bear a broken heart to achieve her goal. But today, with the fall and the bleeding scare, the lie of the land had completely changed.

So now she was stuck with two choices. Leave the baby with Ben, as their deal currently stood, and go on her merry way.

Impossible.

Or stay in their one-sided relationship and raise their child together. And die a little each day.

Also impossible.

But there was a third option. Take the baby and run.

Possible. Plausible. Essential.

But could she do that to Ben? As painful as it was to admit he didn't love her, the same couldn't be said for their baby. Ben was besotted with him. He spent ages each day talking to his son. First thing in the morning and in bed at night he would stroke her stomach and place his lips against her bulge and whisper sweet nothings to it. In two languages.

He talked about the baby non-stop. Told her the things they were going to do together and the places they were going to go and the things he wanted to show his son. At the moment he was going through three different name books, hoping to find a good balance between the baby's Russian and Italian ancestry. He was completely and utterly committed to their baby. Head over heels in love with him. How could she take away the one thing Ben wanted more than anything? The one thing that had started to restore his faith in love? In family?

But how could she stay and keep herself whole? How could she stay and not turn into her mother? This was her dilemma. She couldn't leave her son behind, neither could she stay in a relationship where she was never going to be loved, hoping for some crumbs of affection. She knew Ben was going to be hurt. Angry, probably. But she couldn't stay.

Her childhood memories of her mother's emotional destruction were still too vivid. She'd fought all her life to escape the scars of her upbringing, determined not to repeat her mother's mistakes, and she wouldn't compromise on that because Ben might get hurt in the process.

She could only hope that he had enough compassion in him to understand her motives.

Katya stayed in bed for two days, going slowly stir-crazy. Ben was attentive to a fault which made her cranky and irritable and guilty, knowing what she was about to do to him. She had no further bleeding and the baby was as active as ever. Rocco was pleased with the second scan but cautioned Katya to give up work and take it easy for the rest of her pregnancy.

Katya promised she would and she could see Ben's visible relief in the periphery of her vision. Poor guy. He had taken her moods on the chin the last two days and been the absolute soul of patience. Her heart swelled with love and she felt like a hot knife was being jabbed into her side at the thought of leaving him.

Katya went back to the room and packed her bag, taking only the things she'd arrived with. There was much more stuff she was leaving behind but she had all she needed. Her plane ticket and her clothes. She placed a hand on her stomach—and the baby. Her heart was heavy as she paged Ben.

Ben arrived a few minutes later and she turned and looked at him, her lover, her heart, and tried to memorise every feature. He looked so male and sexy in his scrubs, her chest swelled with love and eyes blurred with tears. If only it didn't have to be this way. If only he could love her like she loved him.

Ben looked at the bag at her feet and the tears shining in her eyes. 'What's all this?'

Katya dashed the tears away and searched for the hard woman who had arrived here some months ago. She'd thought this through enough times in the last two days. Now was the time for action.

'I'm l-leaving.'

Ben stared at her vacantly for a few moments, letting her announcement sink in. He felt as if he'd taken a punch to the solar plexus from a world boxing champion. He felt short of breath. He felt his stomach drop. His mind reeled. What the hell did she mean? 'I'm sorry? What do you mean, you're leaving?'

'I thought I could do this…I really did, Ben. But the other day, when I was bleeding and I thought I was losing the baby, I realised I couldn't. Couldn't walk away from him.'

Ben looked at her earnest face. She didn't want to give the baby up? But that was…perfect. 'So don't,' he said. Ben could tell she was just holding herself together, that one wrong word could see her walking out the door. 'Stay here with me and we'll raise the baby together. My offer of marriage still stands.'

Katya bit her lip to stop the sob that rose in her throat at the casual offer. 'We don't love each other, Ben.' The lie hurt so much she had to gulp in a big breath to ease the pain.

'No, but we love this baby, and that's a good start.'

She stared at him eyes blurry with tears. What had she expected? That he go down on one knee and admit his undying love? She took some deep breaths. How, how could she marry him? She'd never be able to trust his motives. She'd question every aspect of their life together, everything he did, everything he said, not knowing if it was her or the baby motivating him. She couldn't—wouldn't—marry someone who didn't love her.

She shook her head. 'I can't give him up and I can't marry you either.'

Ben felt his heart beat louder in his chest and a slow steady burn rise in his chest. 'So, what? You're just going to leave?' His voice was low and menacing. 'Cut me out of my own child's life? Because you'd better know—I won't take that lying down.'

Katya swiped at a tear that had finally escaped to splash down her cheek. She heard the threat in his voice and knew it wasn't an empty one. She knew he had the power and the means to follow through. Knew that he'd move heaven and earth for his child. 'No. I won't cut you out but I need some time away to think about how we can handle this.'

'Where do you propose to go?'

'London,' she said. It was a good distance but not too far.

Ben could see all his hopes and dreams for the three of them crashing down around him. Katya had been very adamant that she wasn't ever going to be part of their lives, but he had built up that fantasy anyway, convinced she would change her mind. And she had, but she'd also completely changed the rules.

He felt like he had that day with Mario and Bianca. Like the rug had been pulled from under him. 'Like hell you're going to London. You've just had a bleed, it's not safe for you to travel.'

She flinched. Again, his concern for their baby was total. 'Rocco assured me it would be OK to travel.' She had enlisted Gabriella's help as an interpreter after Ben had left.

'No.' Ben shook his head, clenching and unclenching his fists.

Katya raised her chin. 'Are you telling me that you plan to physically restrain me?'

'Don't be ridiculous,' he snapped.

'Then I am going to London.' Katya's heart banged loudly against her ribs. Her hands trembled slightly but she was pleased to see the old strong-as-steel Katya was still there when she needed her.

Ben regarded her seriously, his mind frantically thinking of a legal way to keep her in Italy. Anything he could organise through a court would take a few days. He looked at her stomach full with his child. There had to be a way to keep her here. To convince her to stay.

'I have rights to this baby, too,' he said, injecting steel into his voice.

'I'm not denying you your rights, Ben. Please…I just need some time.' Everything was so mixed up in her head and she couldn't sort it out living here.

Ben could see her torment. Could see this conversation wasn't easy for her either. Maybe some time away would help her see the wisdom of his suggestion? 'How much time?' he demanded.

For ever? 'A few weeks.' She shrugged.

'You can have two.'

Two? She felt like she would do nothing but cry for at least the first two weeks. 'No. Four,' she said.

Ben did a quick calculation in his head. She'd be thirty-six weeks. Still a good month until the baby was born. 'You promise you'll get help if anything else goes wrong with the baby?'

Katya ground her teeth. 'Hell, Ben, of course. Don't worry,

your baby will be well looked after.' *Its mother, on the other hand, will be a mess but don't concern yourself about that.*

'Four weeks, then,' he said, pulling his wallet out of his bedside table drawer, pulling out a credit card and scribbling on a piece of paper. He handed them both to her.

'My card and its PIN number,' he said.

Katya looked at them blankly and then threw them on the bed in disgust. 'I don't want your money, Ben.' She picked up her bag. 'I've never wanted your money.'

She opened the door, unable to believe they were parting like this.

'Keep in touch.'

Katya stilled with her hand on the doorknob, the quiet warning putting a chill up her spine. 'You know my mobile number,' she said, her heart breaking as she walked out of the room without a backward glance.

CHAPTER TEN

Two weeks later, Katya sat in a glass bubble high above the Thames as the London Eye slowly completed a revolution. She hadn't really seen any of the capital spread before her. Big Ben and the Houses of Parliament were directly below her now, but their architectural beauty didn't register. She sat on the central seat staring out aimlessly, while tourists walked around the car, snapping photos.

She didn't even know how she'd ended up here. She'd just had to get out of the flat. Being alone gave her too much time to think, to reflect. To be miserable. She was annoyed with herself that she couldn't just shake it off and that after a fortnight away from Ben she still didn't know what to do.

She yearned desperately for the old Katya to make an appearance. The one who had gone to Italy. The one who had seen her through years of hard times. The one who had ruled her life with an iron fist. But being with Ben, falling in love with him, had softened that woman. His support and understanding had dispensed with the need for her. And furthermore, she couldn't get her back. Loving Ben, having his baby, had changed her for ever.

The ride came to an end and Katya stepped out of the slowly moving car with the other passengers. She pulled her coat collar up and did up the buttons over her baby bump. She was grateful for the warm, knee-length wool as the crisp March air enveloped her. Where to now? She didn't know. Just walk, be among crowds, wander along Oxford Street maybe or around Covent Garden.

Wherever, just not back to the poky little flat in Islington which she was house-sitting for a MedSurg colleague. She almost wished she'd taken Gill and Harriet up on their offer of a bed in Australia. But it was too far away from Ben. And he had made it very clear from his text messages that he wanted to be part of his child's life.

And she knew that if he'd really wanted to play hard ball, he had the money and the means to provide for their son better than she did. And the money and the means to ensure he got his way.

Going back to Italy was inevitable. She knew that deep down. Unless she could persuade Ben to come to London. But ultimately where they lived didn't matter. It still involved seeing him regularly. Seeing him and knowing he could never be hers. Watching him with their child. Maybe even with other women. The newer, softer Katya wasn't strong enough for that.

She was fairly sure, though, that Ben would insist on Italy. He had the Lucia Trust, his pride and joy, still in its infancy, and also his heritage. It may have been one he hadn't wanted but he was embracing it more and more, determined to put his own stamp on it.

So it was either go to Italy willingly or face a court battle for their son. Something she wasn't up to financially or emotionally.

Katya's mobile rang and her heart skipped crazily in her chest. *Ben.* They hadn't spoken since she'd left, communicating by text only.

She flipped the phone open. 'Hello.'

'I'm in London.'

Katya gasped. She wasn't ready yet. Even though every cell in her body ached to see him again. 'I have another two weeks.'

'We need to talk, *cara*.'

Even being brisk and businesslike, his voice was still as sexy as hell. She swallowed.

'I couldn't wait.' His voice was softer this time. She shivered and her toes curled at the sensual, husky purr of his voice. Heaven help her, his voice was stroking all the places that had ached for him this last fortnight.

'Meet me for dinner at seven tonight. One-fifty Piccadilly.'

She heard the disconnected tone and folded the phone away. She should have been annoyed at his presumption but hearing his voice again after so long had obliterated everything. And in a few hours she'd be actually seeing him.

At least he hadn't insisted on coming to the flat. It was small, the entire thing not much bigger than their quarters at the clinic. The bed took up three-quarters of the available room. And they didn't have a very good track record around beds. If she was going to survive with her heart intact, they could never cross that line again.

Ben waited impatiently at the table. She was late. If she didn't show soon he was going to go to her temporary dwelling and drag her out, kicking and screaming. OK, he'd changed the rules but, then, so had she. She couldn't turn his whole world upside down and then just leave and expect him to take it on the chin.

Waking up without her the morning after that fateful day two weeks ago had been the worst moment of his life. Worse than finding his brother making love to his fiancée, worse than the news of Mario's death. Worse than watching her walk out the door. Because he'd realised in that moment, with an empty space in the bed beside him, that he loved her. That he'd fallen in love with her the night they had first made love. He'd just been too stubborn to see it.

And from then on, he'd just been plain mad. The first time he'd risked his heart in a decade and it was being ripped to shreds all over again. It was *déjà vu* and he'd be damned if he would take that sitting down this time. Last time running had been his way of coping. This time he would fight.

But he wouldn't fight for Katya. Yet again it had been proved to him that women only brought heartache. Obviously if she could just walk away from him, she didn't return his feelings. Had only sought him out in Italy when she'd been convinced she couldn't raise the baby herself. To use him.

But he would fight for his child. He'd gone from potentially being a sole parent to no baby at all, and if she thought he'd take that without a fight, like he'd taken Mario and Bianca, then she was wrong. He *would* play a role in this child's life and she either agreed to that or he would make it his life's purpose to seek it through any means at his disposal.

He just wished there was a way to make her love him. That he could take her to court and have a judge order her to love him. But he knew it didn't work like that. That love was either there or it wasn't.

And it obviously wasn't for her. And he was going to have to deal with that for the next however many years. It would be exquisite torture loving her and not being able to tell her. Watching her give birth to their baby. Breast-feeding him. Laughing and talking in Russian to him. Maybe having to put up with another man in her life. In his son's life. It would all be unbearable—but he'd do what he had to do to be a father to his son.

Ben gripped a fork absently, concentrating on his anger. He'd need it to harden his heart. She mustn't know the power she had over him. One woman with the power to crush his heart had been more than enough in his life. And he wouldn't give it to another, not when his child was in the middle.

Because that had to be his focus now. Their child. Their son. This was what being in London was about. To convince her to return to Italy. To hash out a mutually satisfying parental agreement. And if she didn't agree? He'd find a judge to force her to do it.

Katya sat on the back seat of the black cab, watching the lights of London flash by. The taxi pulled up outside the Ritz.

'No, I'm sorry, there must be a mistake,' Katya said, staring at the opulent building. 'I said 150 Piccadilly.'

The taxi driver nodded. 'The Ritz. One-fifty Piccadilly.'

Katya felt her shoulders slump. *Of course. The Ritz. Where else?* She paid him and alighted from the vehicle. It was a chilly night and she hoped she was dressed well enough for such a swanky restaurant.

The doorman opened the heavy gold and glass door for her and she stepped inside nervously, cursing Ben silently. He knew she didn't feel comfortable in places like this. If he'd wanted to put her on the back foot, he had certainly achieved it!

Ben wasn't anywhere in the foyer and she peered into the elegant French-influenced surroundings to see if he was waiting for her further along the vaulted gallery that ran the length of the building.

'Miss Petrova?'

Katya turned to find a concierge in a dark suit with gold braid on his epaulettes addressing her. 'Yes?'

'Count Medici is waiting for you in the dining room,' he said, gesturing down to the end of the gallery.

'Oh, right… Thank you,' she said. It seemed like a very long walk.

'May I take your coat' he asked.

'Ah…yes.' Katya shrugged out of the dark wool. The temperature inside was toasty compared to the chilly night air outside.

Her hands shook and she buried them in her pockets as she walked on equally shaky legs towards the dining room. She passed the elegant Palm Court on her left, where glasses tinkled, crockery clattered and muted laughter mingled with piano music. She continued on until she reached the entrance to the dining room.

'Miss Petrova?' a waiter enquired.

Katya nodded.

'This way, please. The count is expecting you.'

Katya followed the waiter into the glamorous room, her eyes searching the tables, oblivious to the Louis XVI-inspired decor. Her heels sank in to the plush carpet of muted pink, green and cream. Above her head chandeliers linked by gilt garlands cast a subdued glow.

The ceiling from which they hung displayed an amazing fresco. The large floor-to-ceiling windows that faced Green Park were hung with heavy formal drapes. A four-piece band was playing and some couples were dancing.

Katya felt exactly how she'd felt the first time she'd seen inside the Lucia Clinic. Smothered. Stifled. And more and more annoyed. She'd rather be eating a BLT sandwich on a park bench. She felt like she'd been naughty and the principal was summoning her. Trying to impress her with his stature and power.

Trying to intimidate her? Well, she'd never scared easily and if Ben thought he was going to lord it over her, he could think again. She had as much right to this baby as he.

The waiter stopped at a table set for two and pulled out Katya's chair. She ignored it. Ben stared up at her. Her heart slammed madly in her chest. He looked tired and haggard. He had a three-day growth and his jaw looked a little gaunt. He looked utterly gorgeous.

'The Ritz, Ben? How predictable,' Katya saw the waiter discreetly melt away.

'Sarcastic, Katya? How predictable,' he mimicked. 'You're late. Sit.' He could smell cinnamon. She was a sight for sore eyes and as she twisted to sit he saw how much more the swell of her stomach had increased. He suppressed the urge to stand and embrace her, feel her belly pressed against his.

Katya felt rather than saw a waiter pushing her chair under her. Ben ordered a Scotch for himself and some iced water with lemon for her. It irritated her that he hadn't even asked. She wasn't used to seeing him like this. He seemed to be playing Count tonight and she didn't doubt it was another power ploy.

He certainly looked every inch the aristocrat. He was wearing a suit that shrieked of class and money. His shirt was blue with a blue pinstripe and his tie was navy. He looked…wealthy. There was just something about the way he held himself that spoke of old money.

He passed her a menu.

'I'm not hungry,' she said.

He looked at her over the top of the menu. 'I'll have the snails. The signorina will have the quail,' he said, snapping his menu closed and handing it to the waiter.

The last thing Katya wanted to do was sit there and make

small talk over birds and disgusting slugs. She just wanted to get this over with so she could get the hell away. Away from the oppressive opulence in a place she'd never belong. Away from his brooding presence. She'd missed him. So much she ached all over.

'Just say what you need to say, Ben.'

I love you. My life is awful without you. 'What the hell happened to the plan, Katya?'

I fell in love, that's what. With you and our baby. 'I'm sorry,' she said. 'I can't just hand him over to you. I thought I could. Then I took that fall and nearly lost him and I felt so awful, so wretched…I just knew I couldn't give him up.'

'I would never have asked you to.'

No. But you'd ask me to commit to a loveless marriage. 'Once I realised I could do it by myself, I had to get away. It's all this,' she said gesturing around her at the palatial dining room. Waiters with different-coloured jackets fussed over each table under the watchful eye of the head waiter, who wore tails. 'This isn't me, Ben.' It wasn't the real reason but it was another aspect of their relationship that had always made her uneasy.

'It isn't me either,' he denied.

Katya snorted. 'Tonight you look like you were born at this table.'

Ben could feel his patience wearing thin. 'So it was OK for our child to have all this when it was me raising him. But now you want to raise him, all this is too rich for you?'

Oh, God, it sounded so awful when he said it like that. She shook her head. 'You said it yourself, Ben. All a baby really needs is love. It just took me a little while to realise that.'

'Well, whether you like it or not, this child is the heir to the entire Medici fortune, Katya. You think I should let you raise him in some grubby little Islington bedsit?'

Katya gasped. 'How did you...?'

He shrugged. 'As you pointed out, I'm a wealthy person. I have ways.'

The whole time she'd thought he'd been giving her space, respecting her independence, he had known where she was? Had she been watched the entire time? Tonight she was seeing a Ben she didn't like or know. She'd seen glimpses of him in the past, but he was front and centre at the moment.

'What do you want, Ben?' She wanted to get away from him. Every minute she spent in his company was torture. Even through her anger she wanted him to kiss her again.

He regarded her seriously. She sounded tired. He would like nothing better now than to take her up to his suite, undress her and rock her to sleep with his hand cradling her stomach. 'You. Back in Italy. I'll set you up in a flat in Ravello. But we share the parenting half-half. It's that or I take you to court and get full custody. And I will win.'

Katya felt as if he'd thrown knives at her. She knew he was right. What hope did a Russian nurse from a poor background with an average income have against a rich, titled surgeon? Even if she was the mother.

'So I'll be like your kept woman? Like a whore? Like how you offered me a job the morning after we slept together for the first time. Payment for service?'

Ben shut his eyes. He'd known that morning, from her vehement rejection, that he had made a gaffe but he hadn't realised that he'd hurt her quite so much.

'No. I'm sorry, I handled things badly that morning. I didn't mean to make you feel cheap. I was going back to a world and memories I didn't want to confront. I was trying to get my head around all that and I spoke without thinking.'

Katya could hear his sincerity but was too angry to cut him

too much slack. 'I am not my mother,' she said frostily. 'I can get my own place.'

'Don't be ridiculous,' he snapped. 'You're the mother of my child.'

She folded her arms mutinously against her chest. 'You want me back, this is non-negotiable.'

'Places are hideously expensive, Katya.'

'I'll manage,' she said tightly.

Ben realised they could argue the logistics later. The important part was that she was agreeing to return. 'So, you're coming back? And you agree to equal parenting?'

'Yes,' Katya said, removing the napkin that an attentive waiter had placed on her lap and throwing it on the table.

How could she still love him? Because she knew he was just doing whatever it took to be with his baby. Just as she was doing. She had no doubt that he would love and dote on their son with every breath in his body. She felt a streak of jealousy and knew it was wrong. Knew it was twisted.

All the fight suddenly left her. 'I'll be back this time next week. I'll let you know when I'm getting in.'

She stood to leave. There was no point in staying. Her heart was breaking in two and she might just do something stupid, like tell him she loved him.

'Katya.' Ben stood and put a stilling hand on her arm.

He looked at her, trying to read her thoughts. She looked sad and defeated and exhausted. Tears shimmered unshed in her eyes. And something else he couldn't put his finger on. He almost told her then. He hated himself for being so harsh. So cold. All he wanted to do was pull her into his arms. Kiss away the tears. Tell her he loved her. But he couldn't make the words come out of his mouth.

She looked down at where he was holding her arm and he

slowly let her go. She walked away without looking back and he stood and watched her go until her figure completely disappeared from sight.

'Everything OK, Count Medici?' the head waiter asked anxiously.

'No. May I have another Scotch?'

Ben ate his meal. He had won. Why didn't it feel like a victory? Seeing her all pliant and docile had left a bitter taste in his mouth. He preferred the Katya who had first arrived at the table. Maybe once the baby was born and she was too busy to resent him, they could eventually be friends. Even though it would be very hard to pretend there wasn't more.

Hard? It would be impossible. He'd almost told her just then. How long did he think he could hold out? Could he go along loving her from afar for ever? Did he want to? It would kill him, slowly but surely. He knew how it was to hold her, to make love to her. How could he see her every day, want her every day and still stay sane?

That's why he'd left Italy over the Bianca fiasco. Having to face his brother and his ex every day would have been too hard. And his feelings for his long-ago ex were nothing compared to the depth of his feelings for Katya. She had showed him so much in the time he had known her. He had matured and his ability to love had matured, too.

And she had given him the gift of a child and he loved them both dearly. Was he going to let what had happened a decade ago ruin his happiness now? He had let Bianca go, had run. But he was older now, and wiser, and Katya had taught him the meaning of true love. Surely he had to fight for her as well, not just their child?

A woman laughed and Ben looked around. There were a lot of glamorous bejewelled women there that night. But Katya outshone them all. And he'd just let her walk out the door.

His thoughts crystallized for the first time in two weeks. The last time he'd had his heart broken, what had he done? He'd run away. Felt sorry for himself. Played the victim. Well, not this time.

Mario's death had been the catalyst for a lot of change over the last few months. But when he thought about it, it had been Katya's gift that night that had had the most effect on his life. Her recognition of his distress and her unquestioning generosity had shaken and humbled him. He'd fallen in love with her that night.

And not the love of a young man obsessed with perfection and finding the right woman to show off to his brother and the rest of the world, but that of a man with a damaged spirit who had found his soul mate. So, she didn't love him. And that hurt. But it was time to fight for her. To declare his intention of wooing her, wining her over, making her love him.

And in the end, if he failed, then he could hold his head up high and know that he had given it his all. When Bianca had thrown his love back, he'd fled. But Katya wasn't Bianca. Katya wasn't some young man's fancy. She was the woman for him. The only woman for him. A lot had changed in a few short months. And if Bianca and Mario had been alive today, he would have thanked them for their betrayal for it had led him to the woman of his heart. His old bitterness paled into insignificance beside what was now at stake.

He threw back the rest of the contents of his glass, paid his bill and left. It was time to stop running away.

* * *

Katya was lying in bed, crying, when the banging on her door started. She was in her pyjamas, staring unseeingly at the television.

She knew it was him. 'Go away,' she croaked.

'Damn it, Katya, open the door.'

'Go away, Ben. You got what you want. Leave me alone.'

'Katya! So help me, I'm going to break this door down if you don't open it.'

Katya felt another stream of hot tears spill down her face. She believed him. She got up, dabbing at her eyes with a tissue and blowing her nose. She undid the deadbolt and the chain latch and flung the door open.

'Go away,' she yelled at him, and attempted to slam the door in his face. He looked like hell. His tie was gone, his collar unbuttoned, his shirt half hanging out.

Ben brought his arm up to block its closure. 'I need to talk to you and I'm not doing it in the corridor.'

'Afraid you'll catch a disease?' she snapped, and turned on her heel, leaving him standing in the doorway. She got back into bed and pulled the covers up to her chin.

Ben felt a surge of frustration well up inside. Sometimes she was so maddening he wanted to pull her across his knees and smack her bottom.

'You've been crying.'

'Don't flatter yourself,' she said, pointing to the television. 'It's a sad movie.'

'Since when have you cried at movies?' Katya was one of the most unsentimental women he knew.

'Since I got pregnant,' she flared.

Ben picked up the remote from her bedside table and switched the television off.

'I was watching that!'

Ben pulled up a chair and placed it beside the bed. 'Katya, I want to talk to you. I don't want things to be like this between us.'

'Oh, I suppose you want us to be friends after your little threat before?' she sneered. She knew she was being unreasonable but he was so close and he looked so sexy with his hair all tousled and his three-day growth and his shirt half-undone. It had been two weeks and she'd missed him.

'No, I don't want to be your friend.'

'Well, that won't—'

'Katya, shut up,' Ben interrupted harshly. 'I have something to say and I'd really appreciate if you could just keep your shrewish tongue still until I've finished. Do you think you can do that?' he demanded.

Katya blinked at his masterful tone. 'Do you promise to leave as soon as it's said?' she asked.

He sighed. 'Yes.' Ben figured she'd probably turf him out anyway.

'OK, then,' she said, drawing her knees up and placing her hands protectively across her abdomen.

Now he had the opportunity he wasn't sure where to start. 'I realized something big recently, after you'd gone. I realised that I loved you.' Katya opened her mouth to speak and he held up his hand and shot her a warning look.

'I was angry, too, of course. In fact, it's been anger that has got me through this last two weeks. Because I realised that it was all one-sided. Because if you loved me, you wouldn't have taken my baby away.'

Katya tried to interject again but again he hushed her. 'It was like Bianca all over again. Loving someone who didn't love me back. And that hurt and it brought back some painful memories. But it's worse this time around because I was so immature last time. I didn't know the true meaning of love. I was selfish. Thinking that it was all about me and my feelings. You helped me see that it wasn't some great conspiracy against me, that things like that happen in life sometimes. You showed me a mature form of love. A selfless love. By letting me seek solace in your body when I needed it so badly, even though you were a virgin, and by being willing to give up your baby because you didn't think you'd be a fit mother.'

Katya's hands trembled as his words sunk in. He loved her? Was it possible? Her heart thundered in her ears. She lay stock still waiting for the but.

'But…'

Katya held her breath, waiting to hear how her running off and her behaviour tonight had totally destroyed his love.

'Tonight I decided I wasn't going to lie down and take it like I did with Bianca. I've decided I'm going to fight for it. I know you don't love me back, that you may never love me, but I'm declaring my intention to woo you.'

'But—'

Ben held up his hand again. 'I know my whole lifestyle makes you uncomfortable. But I can't change who I am, Katya. I know that because I spent a lot of years fighting it. And it was you who made me see that I could be the version of me that I wanted to be, not the one everyone expected. And this title allows me to do so much more good in this world. But I don't need or care for any of its trappings. We'll stay home every night and eat bruschetta from Taddeo's if it means that you'll grow to love me.'

'Ben—'

He shook his head. 'No. I haven't finished yet. And if you never love me, at least I'll know that I tried and that there'll be honesty between us. Because if we're going to raise this child separately, we're going to need that.'

Katya felt tears build in her eyes and one roll down her cheek. He had said the words she had never thought she'd hear from his mouth.

'What about Bianca? Don't you still love her?'

Ben rubbed his hands through his hair. 'No, no, no. I've been hanging onto my bitterness not because I still love her but to protect myself from getting hurt again. I was a fool. You're the one I love. You were right there in front of me and I didn't realise it until you were gone. I'd been so used to emotional isolation I didn't recognise that you'd brought me back into the fold.'

Katya felt the baby move beneath her hands. He gave her a couple of hefty kicks and she grimaced. She looked at Ben, his face so earnest, so hopeful. She picked up his hand off his knee, brought it across and laced it under hers down low on her bump where the baby was partying.

Ben felt the strong movements and dropped to his knees beside the bed, burying his face against her abdomen, his cheek resting against the bulge. He kissed her gently there, where the baby was somersaulting, and cinnamon suffused his senses. He wanted to pull back the bedclothes, remove her pyjamas and just stare at her pregnant body. He had missed her so much.

Katya stared at his downturned head. Felt his lips sear her abdomen even through layers of bed linen and pyjamas. Her heart swelled with love. She had put him through hell. 'Do you remember the moment?' she asked quietly, her hand creeping down to push involuntarily through his hair.

Ben looked up at her. 'What moment?'

'That you fell in love with me.'

Ben nodded. 'The night we made love for the first time. I didn't realise it at the time but, looking back, I know I've loved you since that night.'

Katya smiled. 'Me, too.'

Ben stilled. 'You, too?'

Katya nodded. 'I didn't realise it until the night we made love at the villa. But I fell hard for you the night Mario and Bianca were killed. You were so devastated, so intense, so… different. You flipped the switch on every feminine cell I possessed that night.'

He grinned slowly. 'It was an amazing night. I'm so sorry about the next morning.'

'Don't,' she said dismissively. 'I reacted badly, too. I was angry with myself for being so irresponsible, so like my mother.'

They grinned at each other for a few more moments, letting the revelations sink in.

'Hop up,' Katya said, moving slightly and displacing Ben from his position.

Ben straightened up and looked at her questioningly. He'd liked that spot. She pulled back the covers and held them open for him.

'Well?' she said. 'You want to get closer?'

Ben grinned at her. He stood and shucked his shoes off and then joined her under the covers, fully clothed. She went into his arms eagerly and with her head against the steady thump of his heart, she knew she was where she wanted to be for ever.

'I'm sorry about these last two weeks, Ben. Once I realised I couldn't give up the baby, I couldn't stay. I didn't want to live with a man who could never love me back.'

'Hush,' he said revelling in their bodies pressed together again. 'I know. I understand. I didn't know how I was going to face you every day either, knowing I loved you. Knowing you didn't love me.'

Katya sighed. What fools they'd both been. 'I love you, Ben.'

He looked down into her eyes. 'I love you too, Katya. Marry me?'

She looked at him solemnly. 'Anywhere. Any time.'

Ben lowered his head and captured her mouth with his. He could taste her tears as they tracked down her face and mingled with their meshed lips. 'Don't cry,' he whispered. 'I'm going to make you happier than you've ever been in your life. And it starts right now.'

As his head swooped again, Katya heard the conviction and sincerity in his voice and gave herself up to his delicious promise.

EPILOGUE

KATYA reclined back against the pillows, weary but content, Mario Ivan Medici snuggled in her arms, sleeping peacefully. His cherubic face was gorgeous, his features a mirror image of his father's.

Ben, sitting on the chair beside the bed, smiled at her—the most beautiful woman in the whole world. Watching her give birth to their son had been the most humbling experience of his life and he bowed to the amazing power and control of his wife-to-be.

He pulled a flat square leather box out of his inner jacket pocket and handed it to her. Katya looked at it without touching it, noticed the company motif and felt tears well in her eyes. Her heartbeat picked up its tempo. She could hear the sound of her breathing loud in her ears.

He opened the box for her and she gave a soft gasp, even though she'd known the minute he'd produced it what the box contained. The cameo they'd fought over sat nestled in the silky lining.

Ben could see the play of emotions across her face. The same look he'd seen in the shop that day. A glimpse of the little girl she'd been before she'd lost her childhood. A glimpse of the yearning that she'd suppressed so hard.

He'd had the cameo attached to a two-strand red coral choker and he lifted it over her head and placed it around her neck. She didn't protest, just sat very still while he latched it at her nape.

She brought her fingers up slowly to stroke the delicate chalky white carving of the curly-haired woman with the bare shoulders and sad smile. It felt firm around her neck but also, strangely, like it belonged there. Katya felt an instant connection with her grandmother and knew she would treasure it for ever.

'Thank you,' she said quietly, her eyes meeting his. 'It's beautiful.'

'I want you to wear it on our wedding day,' he said.

Tears shimmered in her blue eyes. 'I'll wear it with pride.'

He dropped a kiss on her blonde head and she raised her face to claim another on her mouth. The baby stirred and Katya broke off, hushing and rocking him gently.

'We were supposed to speak to the mayor today,' Katya said after her son had settled. 'Do you think he'll reschedule?'

Ben chuckled. 'I think when he knows we were a little busy, he'll fit us in another time. He's as eager to marry us as we are to marry each other, *cara*.'

'What about the sundial? Will that be done by the wedding date?' she asked.

Ben eased out of his seat and went to the balcony and looked down at the gardens, the Med sparkling like a jewel in the distance. Two workmen were installing the heavy masonry ornament down on the bottom tier of the garden.

Ben had decided to honour his brother with a sundial. It had been the one thing Mario had always wanted to see in the garden and had never got around to doing. The process had been cathartic, to say the least.

Their wedding was taking place next to the sundial, and

Ben felt like he was finally claiming the gardens for himself while still acknowledging his brother's contribution. Both to the gardens and his life. And he had Katya to thank for it.

'They'll be finished tomorrow,' he said.

He walked back into the room and sat back on the chair.

'Did you speak with your mother?'

Katya smiled at him and nodded. 'She and Dimitri are both coming.' That her mother had married two months ago had come as a complete surprise. That a bridge had finally been built between mother and daughter, even more so. It was new and rickety, and Katya wasn't sure they'd ever be really close, but she'd never heard her mother so content, and it was a start. Katya knew she had Ben to thank for it. 'They arrive at the weekend.'

In fact, thanks to Ben, her whole family was going to attend the wedding. Sophia, Anna and Marisha were all going to be bridesmaids.

Katya linked her spare hand with his and they both sat watching their newborn son sleep.

'Thank you,' Ben said. 'Thank you for making me the happiest man in the world.'

Katya smiled at Ben, her heart filling with joy and love. 'Thank you,' she replied. 'For him. For this.' She touched her cameo. 'For being patient. For helping me reconnect with my mother. For loving me.'

Ben rose and kissed Katya lightly on the mouth. 'I'm going to spend the rest of my life loving you.'

And then he kissed her properly. Today was a wonderful day. His son was healthy. Katya was happy. The Lucia Trust was thriving. Life was perfect. Just as they both deserved.

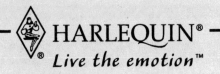

HARLEQUIN®

Live the emotion™

American ★ Romance®

Heart, Home & Happiness

HARLEQUIN®

Blaze™

Red-hot reads.

Harlequin® Historical
Historical Romantic Adventure!

HARLEQUIN®

HARLEQUIN ROMANCE®

From the Heart, For the Heart

HARLEQUIN®

INTRIGUE®

Breathtaking Romantic Suspense

Medical Romance™...
love is just a heartbeat away

HARLEQUIN®
Presents~
Seduction and Passion Guaranteed!

HARLEQUIN®
Super Romance®

Exciting, Emotional, Unexpected

www.eHarlequin.com

HDIR08

HARLEQUIN ROMANCE®

The rush of falling in love,

Cosmopolitan,
international settings,

Believable, feel-good stories
about today's women

The compelling thrill
of romantic excitement

It could happen to you!

EXPERIENCE
HARLEQUIN ROMANCE!

Available wherever Harlequin Books are sold.

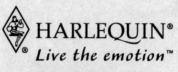

HARLEQUIN®
Live the emotion™

www.eHarlequin.com

HROMDIR04

HARLEQUIN®

American ROMANCE®

Invites *you* to experience lively, heartwarming all-American romances

Every month, we bring you four strong, sexy men, and four women who know what they want—and go all out to get it.

From small towns to big cities, experience a sense of adventure, romance and family spirit—the all-American way!

American ROMANCE
Heart, Home & Happiness

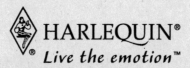

HARLEQUIN®
Live the emotion™

www.eHarlequin.com   HARDIR06

HARLEQUIN®
INTRIGUE®

BREATHTAKING ROMANTIC SUSPENSE

Shared dangers and passions lead to electrifying
romance and heart-stopping suspense!

Every month, you'll meet six new heroes
who are guaranteed to make your spine tingle
and your pulse pound. With them you'll enter
into the exciting world of Harlequin Intrigue—
where your life is on the line
and so is your heart!

THAT'S INTRIGUE—
ROMANTIC SUSPENSE
AT ITS BEST!

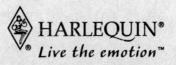

HARLEQUIN®
Live the emotion™

www.eHarlequin.com   INTDIR06

HARLEQUIN®

Super Romance®

...there's more to the story!

Superromance.
A *big* satisfying read about unforgettable
characters. Each month we offer *six* very different
stories that range from family drama to adventure
and mystery, from highly emotional stories to
romantic comedies—and much more! Stories
about people you'll believe in and care about.
Stories too compelling to put down....

Our authors are among today's *best* romance
writers. You'll find familiar names and talented
newcomers. Many of them are award winners—
and you'll see why!

If you want the biggest and best
in romance fiction, you'll get it
from Superromance!

Exciting, Emotional, Unexpected...

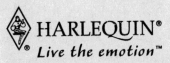

HARLEQUIN®
Live the emotion™

www.eHarlequin.com   HSDIR06

HARLEQUIN®
Presents

The world's bestselling romance series...
The series that brings you your favorite authors,
month after month:

Helen Bianchin...Emma Darcy
Lynne Graham...Penny Jordan
Miranda Lee...Sandra Marton
Anne Mather...Carole Mortimer
Melanie Milburne...Michelle Reid

and many more talented authors!

Wealthy, powerful, gorgeous men...
Women who have feelings just like your own...
The stories you love, set in exotic, glamorous locations...

HARLEQUIN®
Presents

Seduction and Passion Guaranteed!

HPDIR08

www.eHarlequin.com

Harlequin® Historical
Historical Romantic Adventure!

Imagine a time of chivalrous knights and unconventional ladies, roguish rakes and impetuous heiresses, rugged cowboys and spirited frontierswomen— these rich and vivid tales will capture your imagination!

Harlequin Historical... they're too good to miss!

Silhouette

SPECIAL EDITION™

Emotional, compelling stories that capture the intensity of living, loving and creating a family in today's world.

Special Edition features bestselling authors such as Susan Mallery, Sherryl Woods, Christine Rimmer, Joan Elliott Pickart— and many more!

For a romantic, complex and emotional read, choose Silhouette Special Edition.

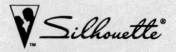

Silhouette®

Visit Silhouette Books at www.eHarlequin.com   SSEGEN06